MAGORA

HOLLY O'FLANIGAN

MAGORA

THE GALLERY OF WONDERS

BOOK ONE

 MARC REMUS

MISTY MOON
BOOKS

First published 2016 by Misty Moon Books

Copyright © 2016 Marc Remus
Illustrations © 2016 Marc Remus

www.MarcRemus.com/author

Cover design and illustrations by Marc Remus
Designed and typeset by Marc Remus

Editor-in-Chief: Nancy Butts
Associate editors: Cheryl Zach, Crystal Watanabe
Copy editor: Marlo Garnsworthy
Volume editor: Ardath Mayhar

Magora - Book 1 (1 of 6) - The Gallery of Wonders

Summary:
When eleven year-old Holly falls into a fantasy painting, she embarks on a thrilling adventure in the parallel world of Magora. There, she must learn to weave painting with magic to survive the threat of the Unfinished—monstrous beings created when an artist leaves a painting incomplete.

ISBN: 978-3-00-051930-7 (Paperback)
ISBN: 978-3-00-051952-9 (ebook)

For Sofia, who inspired me to create Holly.
You will always be the heart of Magora.

CONTENTS

Chapter 1: The Fire   9

Chapter 2: The Mysterious Box   19

Chapter 3: The Hidden Attic   31

Chapter 4: The Gate   39

Chapter 5: Gindars   47

Chapter 6: The Wall of Gors   55

Chapter 7: The Trip to the Hatchery   63

Chapter 8: Cookie the Troll   69

Chapter 9: Villa Nonesuch   75

Chapter 10: The Prophecy   81

Chapter 11: Creation and Deletion Brushstrokes   87

Chapter 12: Cliffony, Academy of the Arts   95

Chapter 13: The Exam   105

Chapter 14: Oracle Gullveig   111

Chapter 15: The Tower of Bats   119

Chapter 16: Ravenscraig Lane   127

Chapter 17: Professor Lapia's Class   135

Chapter 18: Professor Farouche's Class   145

Chapter 19: The Unfinished   153

Chapter 20: The Ward   161

Chapter 21: The Secret Tunnel   169

Chapter 22: The Gallery of Wonders   175

Chapter 23: Time Wasted   183

Chapter 24: Detention   189

Chapter 25: The Flower of Creativity   199

Chapter 26: The Quadrennial Art Competition   205

Chapter 27: Villa Littlemore   211

Chapter 28: Cuspidor's Accomplice   219

Chapter 29: Chaos   225

Chapter 30: Burma   231

Chapter 31: Cuspidor's True Nature   241

Chapter 32: Saying Goodbye   247

The Fire

The line between reality and fantasy has many shapes. It can be thick or thin, colorful or dull, wavy or straight, blurry or sharp. It is always changing.

The smell of burning wood woke Holly from a restless sleep in the attic. She leaped from her crouched position on the dirty mattress to the window above. Something was on fire.

Holly flung the window open and saw flames. Smoke poured in, creating a hazy fog that hung in the dark, dreary room. She coughed, wiping the hair away from her face. The fire was close to Grandpa Nikolas' house. What if something had happened to him?

She ran to the crammed shelves that lined the staircase leading down to the third floor. They were stuffed to the ceiling with cans of paint, rusty lanterns, baskets full of Christmas decorations, and many other useless things. She hoisted one of the paint cans aside and picked up a pair of binoculars.

Another cloud of smoke blew into the attic as she rushed back to the window. Coughing, she frantically waved her hands to scatter the smoke. Holly focused the binoculars on Papplewick Road. She couldn't see exactly where the fire was, but she noticed that the flames were shooting to the sky from behind the house of Ms. Hubbleworth, a neighbor known for being a nosy busybody.

"I need to warn everybody," Holly said, panicked.

She dropped the binoculars into her backpack, grabbed a coat, and hurried down the attic staircase. To her surprise, her foster parents, the Smoralls, hadn't locked her in as they usually did in the evening.

Holly raced down the marble hallway of the Smoralls' luxurious mansion and dashed into the kitchen.

"There's a fire," she cried breathlessly.

A red-haired girl sat on a chair, munching on a towering stack of chocolate cookies. Though the Smoralls' daughter Barb was, at age thirteen, only two years older than Holly, she was about twice her weight. Hundreds of freckles covered her flat face, which had a strong resemblance to that of an orangutan.

"Mom, the loser is down from the attic," Barb said.

Ms. Smorall turned away from the counter where she had been kneading dough. She wiped her hands on an oversized apron that hid her thinness.

"What are you doing down here?" Ms. Smorall scolded. She dropped the dough onto the kitchen table and moved

menacingly toward Holly, finger pointed. "I have not given you permission to leave the attic." She pulled Holly up by one ear.

"I'm sorry," Holly pleaded. "But there's a fire. Someone might be in danger."

Ms. Smorall glared at Holly with beady eyes as she pulled her closer. Holly's face almost touched her foster mother's crooked nose.

"She's such a loser," said Barb as she stuffed two cookies into her mouth at the same time. "Guess what her teacher, Mr. MacMillan, said last week?"

Ms. Smorall lifted her razor-thin eyebrows and smiled. "What did he say, sweetie?"

"Holly painted a line with two circles and tried to pass it off as a flying rabbit and a magical carriage," Barb said.

Ms. Smorall broke out in a hysterical laugh. "A flying rabbit? That's ridiculous. You have no talent whatsoever when it comes to art."

"Who has no talent?" asked a red-haired man with the same orangutan features as Barb. He strolled into the kitchen and went to the refrigerator.

"H-h-herbert, I didn't expect you to be home this early," Ms. Smorall stuttered in a slightly irritated tone.

"I got off early today," Mr. Smorall said as he grabbed a can of soda from the refrigerator. He turned to Barb. "And how is my sweetheart doing?"

At that moment, Ms. Smorall pushed Holly out into the hallway. "Don't you ever dare come down here again, or I will make you clean the whole mansion with a toothbrush," she whispered harshly before giving Holly another push.

Holly stumbled backward as Ms. Smorall let go of her ear. There was no doubt that Ms. Smorall really would make her clean the mansion with a toothbrush. Holly was already forced to do all the chores in the house and Ms. Smorall used every opportunity to humiliate Holly. Holly never understood why.

"Up into the attic now," Ms. Smorall snapped. She slammed the kitchen door shut.

Holly rubbed her ear, which hurt where Ms. Smorall had yanked on it. She dashed down the marble hallway to the front door, flung it open, and ran along Piddlehinton Street.

She knew she would be punished for not going back into the attic, but it was much more important to make sure Grandpa Nikolas was all right.

A burning smell hung in the air, and she saw the flickering of flames in the distance. Just as she passed Ms. Hubbleworth's house, a boy around Holly's age came running around the corner.

He swerved around a lamppost, slipped, and crashed headfirst into a puddle of mud. His oval glasses disappeared into the brown goop in front of him. He fished them out, rubbed them on his mud-covered turtleneck, and stared horror-struck at the fire.

"Brian," Holly said, rushing over to him. "Are you okay?"

"I'm good," said Brian. "Did you see? There's a fire in the building where your grandpa has his art studio."

"I know," Holly said, her heart beating so fast it felt as if it were about to break through her ribcage. If anything happened to Grandpa Nikolas, she would be left without any family. Even though Holly was not allowed to visit him because of rumors

that he was practicing some kind of magical rituals, she still thought about him all the time.

"Come on," said Brian, wiping the dirt from his turtleneck. "Let's see what's going on."

A few moments later, Holly and Brian reached Grandpa Nikolas' studio. Hundreds of people had gathered in the street, looking up at the flames lightening the dark sky. In the distance, Holly heard the sirens of fire trucks approaching.

"Grandpa Nikolas' studio is up there on the top floor," Holly said, aghast, as she watched flames shooting out of the upper floor windows. "I have to get him out."

"We can't go in there," Brian said, pointing at the crowd of people who had already ran from the burning building. "They all escaped just in time. I'm sure Grandpa Nikolas has already left."

"And if he hasn't, it wouldn't be much of a loss," said a voice behind Holly.

She turned around and looked into a wrinkled face with thick pinkish makeup. Perched on top of a beehive of blonde hair was a sunhat with pink pompons that matched the pink outfit the woman was wearing.

"Hubbleworth." Holly rolled her eyes and whispered to Brian, "She looks like a plastic flamingo."

"He's a madman, just like every painter," said Ms. Hubbleworth. "No wonder the court decided to take you away from him."

"Grandpa Nikolas is not a madman," said Holly. "He's a very creative painter, and they didn't take me away because he's crazy, but because someone spread lies about him."

"Stop bugging her," Brian said. "Everybody knows you hate kids, so why don't you just ignore us?"

"Very right, Mr. Findley. You are nothing but little pests."

"I bet you were the one who spread those rumors about Holly's grandfather," Brian said accusingly.

"Strange things were taking place at Nikolas O'Flanigan's studio," said Ms. Hubbleworth. "I wish they had taken him away from Donkleywood and not just separated him from Holly."

Holly wanted to strangle Ms. Hubbleworth, but forced herself to stay calm.

She knew there were a lot of rumors in town about her grandfather, but she had never believed any of them. However, she knew how much Ms. Hubbleworth despised the idea of anything that did not fit into her small world, including magic. There was no doubt in Holly's mind that the old lady had something to do with the rumors.

Brian pulled Holly away from Ms. Hubbleworth and away from the crowd to a tiny park across from the building. Holly climbed onto one of the benches and took the binoculars out of her backpack. She focused them on the upper floor.

"I need to go," Brian said, heading toward the bushes.

"Go where?"

"To the bathroom," he called back.

"Really?" Holly asked incredulously. "In the bushes?"

As she waited for Brian to return, she scanned the crowd standing in front of the building. She was hoping to find Grandpa Nikolas, but there was no sign of him. Trembling, she lowered the binoculars and turned back to the park. Where was

THE GALLERY OF WONDERS

Brian? It couldn't be taking him this long to do his business.

Her eyes had slowly adjusted to the darkness of the park when she spotted Brian hiding behind a bush. He was pointing at a nearby thick oak tree while signaling her to be quiet.

Holly focused her binoculars on the tree that was about sixty feet away. Something was moving between its crooked branches. Was it a crow or a cat? It was too dark to see, and she couldn't make out the shadowy figure. Holly flipped the binoculars over and cleaned the lenses on her sweater. As she focused again, three pairs of eyes stared right at her.

"Crows," Holly said, unimpressed.

At that precise moment, a bright flame shot up from the fire and lit the treetop. For one second, Holly saw clearly. Those were no crows. Her heart turned over. She lost her balance, dropped the binoculars, and fell off the bench.

"S-s-seahorses?" Holly stuttered as she lay on the ground.

Had she actually seen flying seahorses in the tree? Holly jumped back up on her feet and grabbed the binoculars. Jittery, she focused them. There they were, three seahorses as big as cats, but they weren't ordinary seahorses. Their leathery tails were spiked with gigantic steel needles, and their bodies were protected by rusted armor. Metal helmets covered their heads and smoke steamed from their snouts. Their bulgy eyes gazed at Holly as if they could see her from the distance.

Holly saw Brian tiptoeing behind the bushes toward the oak tree. Just as Brian was about to reach the thick trunk, Holly realized that something else was moving in the dark. She focused the binoculars again. Her heart was pounding as she searched the darkness.

A short bald man with a pockmarked face and a thin, black moustache was hiding behind the trunk. A thick, fleshy scar ran all around his unnaturally elongated head. A purple cloak with a ruff hung loosely over his velvet pants, which were tucked into his boots. They were oddly curled at the front, just like snail shells. Holly had never seen a costume like that before—except in paintings depicting wizards from medieval times. The man was talking to himself while pointing at the seahorses above him.

Brian tiptoed closer to the odd man and hid behind another bush.

Another burst of flame flooded the area with bright orange light. Holly's hands started to shake and she cried out at what she saw next.

A creature, about seven feet tall, stood behind the man. It was draped in a black cloak and a hood was pulled over its face. Not an inch of flesh was visible. The image of the Grim Reaper came to Holly's mind.

Who were these people? Did they have something to do with the fire? Holly saw Brian signaling her to come over.

Holly tiptoed to the oak tree, carefully hiding behind the bushes along the way.

"Who are they?" she whispered when she reached Brian.

"This is so weird," he said. "I think those people are after the flying seahorses up there." He pointed at the treetop where the odd creatures still hovered.

"Do you think these people have anything to do with the fire?" Holly asked. "Maybe they are arsonists?"

Brian shrugged. "Just listen to what they're saying."

Holly crawled on her hands and knees, moving closer to the base of the oak until she could clearly see the man with the scar.

"We're running out of time," said the man. "We need to find the Gindar."

The cloaked creature behind the man nodded.

What on earth was a Gindar? Holly had never heard the word before.

"We have to bring the seahorses back," said the man. "And we need to get Holly O'Flanigan quickly."

Holly froze as soon as she heard her name. She pressed her hand over her mouth, fearful of letting out a sound.

These people were after her. But why? Why would anybody be after her? She didn't have anything that was valuable. She hadn't done anything wrong either, at least as far as she knew. So what would anybody want with her?

A scream echoed through the park. Startled, Holly looked back over her shoulder. She knew that voice. Panicked, she crawled back, jumped up, and ran past Brian, completely forgetting her need to be quiet.

As she reached the edge of the park, she looked up and saw Grandpa Nikolas standing on the roof of the building. He was surrounded by flames. Holly realized, with a horrible pang in her stomach, he was about to jump to try to escape them.

"No, don't do it!" Holly screamed. "The firefighters will be here soon!"

As if to confirm her words, the wail of sirens from the approaching fire trucks grew louder. But they weren't close enough. Grandpa Nikolas screamed one more time. Then, he leaped toward the edge of the roof and, as the crowd shouted from the street below, he jumped.

The Mysterious Box

The line can be thick or thin. It all depends how thick you make it. There were years in my childhood when fantasy and reality were the same thing. The line was wafer-thin, almost nonexistent. At other times, fantasy was overshadowed by everyday reality, and the line was so thick it was almost impossible to let fantasy be a part of my life.

Holly spent half of the night staring up at the ceiling, her eyes flooded with tears. Grandpa Nikolas was dead. Holly couldn't get the horrible picture of her grandfather jumping off the building out of her mind. She knew the panicked look on his face would haunt her for the rest of her life. But even though Grandpa Nikolas was gone, Holly's life continued. And now she would have to live with the Smoralls forever. Even though they were the only distant relatives she had, Holly would never find a real home with them.

"Don't ever forget that you have creativity inside you," Grandpa Nikolas had said years ago, just before Holly was taken away from him. "You can become a good painter like me."

But even though Holly wanted to become a great painter, she knew the Smoralls would never allow that. All they saw in her drawings were scribbles. And many students at her school thought so too. Amanda Heavenlock was one of them. She was the prettiest of all the girls in her class and a year older than Holly. Amanda constantly made fun of Holly by calling her the Scribble Queen. True, for most people her drawings didn't look like anything but that was why Holly wanted to go to Brushdale Art School, a school specializing in the arts.

Now all her dreams were shattered. The only person in the family who had supported her dreams was now dead. Holly cried herself to sleep.

It was still dark when Holly woke the next morning. She was exhausted. All night long she had dreamed of Grandpa Nikolas. She got up from the mattress and walked down the attic staircase. She crouched down and pushed against the wood on the front of the fourth step to reveal a secret cubbyhole. She squeezed her hand in, sifted through the dust inside the step, and pulled out an old cigar case she had hidden there. It was made of polished silver and engraved with the name "O'Flanigan."

Holly dusted it off and caressed the case, then gently opened the lid. A few dozen photos were neatly stacked on the red velvet lining. The photo on top showed three people, a friendly-looking man with a short white beard stood to the right. It was Grandpa Nikolas in his sixties. On his right arm was a pretty woman with wiry blonde curls. A Mediterranean-looking man with thick, jet-black eyebrows and a long face stood beside her. Grandpa Nikolas had told Holly that these were her parents. She had never known them because they had died in an accident when she was a baby.

Tears rolled down Holly's cheeks. "I want a family and a home like everybody else," she whispered, wiping her tears on her sleeves. "Grandpa Nikolas, please come back. You were the only family I had left."

She gently set aside the photos of Grandpa Nikolas and pulled out a few sheets of paper from the box. The sheet on the front read:

How Butterflies Live, Reproduce, and Fly
Research Paper by Holly O'Flanigan
5th Grade Science Project.

It was this final research paper on butterflies that had saved Holly from failing science class and therefore the entire school year. She had already flunked art. Despite her passion for painting, Mr. McMillan had failed her because he didn't recognize anything Holly drew. And failing two classes would have meant repeating a year.

Failing art was bad enough; two classes would have been too much. But the science teacher gave her the chance to write a paper, pass science, and move to sixth grade. Even though the Smoralls had tried to keep Holly from studying by overwhelming her with chores, she had snuck out to the library and was able to finish the paper on time.

As Holly placed the photos and the paper back in the box, she heard someone call her name. She went up the stairs and opened the window.

Holly smiled. It was her friend, Rufus. His short red hair and the freckles that went with it almost looked orange in the morning light. As usual, he was dressed in the blue post office uniform he wore while helping out his parents who ran the Donkleywood post office. Rufus' skinny body barely supported the weight of the heavy woolen coat he was wearing over his outfit.

"I am so sorry for what happened to your grandfather," he said in a fake British accent. Rufus was very intelligent and liked to show it. Over time, he had gotten into the habit of imitating the accent, which he thought made him sound more sophisticated.

"Thank you, Rufus," said Holly, as she watched him pull out a rather large box from underneath the trimmed boxwood bushes.

"What do you have there?" Holly asked.

"I have a package for you," Rufus said. "Please lower the basket."

Holly threw down a basket while holding the rope attached to it. Rufus placed the box in the basket and gave her a signal to pull it up.

"When I left the post office, I found this on the doorstep," he said. "It's quite odd. Nobody had taken it inside to mail. It was just lying there, addressed to you."

"That's weird," said Holly, pulling on the rope until it was

taut, then began hauling it up. "Why would someone leave a box for me in front of the post office?"

"Whoever sent it to you must have known the Smoralls would not give it to you if it arrived by regular mail," Rufus said.

"I guess you're right."

Holly leaned back and yanked on the rope as if she were playing tug-of-war. "Jeepers, that's heavy," she grumbled.

With a clunk, the box landed on the windowsill and dropped to the floor. A lilac envelope was attached to it.

"I have to go back to the post office," Rufus called.

"All right," said Holly. "Thanks, Rufus."

He disappeared between the bushes, and Holly closed the window.

"Strange—no sender," she said to herself, flipping the box upside-down.

Holly kneeled on the dirty mattress that Ms. Smorall had gotten from a garbage dump. She placed the box on her pillow and picked up the lilac envelope. It read:

To: Gindar Holly O'Flanigan
13 Piddlehinton Street
Donkleywood

"Gindar?" Holly jumped up from the mattress. She remembered the scarred man, who had mentioned that word before. Did he and the cloaked creature send this box? Holly held the envelope at arm's length as if it contained a bomb ready to explode. But, curious as she was, she couldn't resist for long. She opened it. A scribbled note read:

Dear Holly:
Take good care of Tenshi. There are some things in the box you
might need in the future. Be careful! Good luck!

No signature. That was very strange. And who was Tenshi? Holly stuffed the letter in her pocket and opened the box.

Inside, she found a leather-bound book, a red feather that split symmetrically into two on the top that looked like conjoined twins, a little jar of white powder, and a gadget with a funnel attached to one side. The book had a coat of arms on its cover. Two eagle-headed lions intertwined with a paintbrush in between them were embossed on the binding. Holly read the medieval lettering on the cover.

Encyclopedia of Magora ~ by Samuel E. Thorvalor.
A complete 80,000-year historical guide.

Holly turned the book around and read the back cover.

This volume includes a special section about creation of Ledesmas
and the battle against S.A. Lokin, Duke of Cuspidor.

"Magora?" Holly mumbled to herself. "What on earth is Magora?"

She read the title again and stopped at the number eighty-thousand. This must have been a printing mistake. No place in the world was that old. She flipped through the pages, fascinated

by the fine illustrations. Each page contained a summary of a few hundred years that together made up the entire history of a place named Magora. It was not a printing mistake. Magora was an eighty-thousand-year-old land.

Puzzled, she set the book aside and read the label on the little jar: *Mind-Splitting Powder—Use With Caution.*

She opened the jar. The smell of moldy mushrooms and rotten eggs filled the air. "Yuck," she said, wrinkling her nose.

She screwed the lid back on tightly, placed the jar on her pillow, and lifted the box with the funnel. She had never seen anything like it. Shaped like an old rotary telephone, it had a funnel instead of a dial. On the opposite side was a hole. An inscription on the bottom read:

Shrink-O-Meter – For professional use only.
Do not use without permission from the High Council.
Instructions:
1. Place object in funnel.
2. Push green button.
3. Move lever upward. Object will shrink.
4. For reversal, push red button.

Holly immediately grabbed a tube of oil paint from a tackle box that Grandpa Nikolas had given her long ago. She placed it in the funnel. Skeptically, she followed the instructions and waited. Nothing happened.

"I knew it," she said, satisfied. "It's a hoax."

At that precise moment, the green button flashed. A huge green cloud blew out of the funnel and filled the room with an icy fog. Holly dropped the Shrink-O-Meter on the mattress and leaped behind the wardrobe.

"Jeepers, what was that?" she shouted.

A gurgling sound came from the funnel. Like a vacuum cleaner, the Shrink-O-Meter sucked in the tube of paint. After a high-pitched microwave-like ding, something small was ejected from the hole.

The fog gradually dissipated. Holly tiptoed up to the Shrink-O-Meter. The tube was lying on the mattress, but now it was no larger than a fingernail. Holly rubbed her eyes in disbelief. Had the Shrink-O-Meter actually shrunk the tube?

Unconvinced, she put the miniature tube back into the funnel, pushed the red button, and hit the lever. Once again, the Shrink-O-Meter blew out fog, sucked the tube in, and with a ding, the tube dropped back out—this time in its original size.

"Wow," Holly said in amazement. Who could have sent her this stuff? She had to show this to Brian and Rufus.

She began shrinking each of the objects from the box so they would all fit in her backpack and carefully placed them inside. Just as she had finished shrinking the encyclopedia, she heard a tapping. She jumped up from her mattress and stood quietly, listening. The gurgling of the Shrink-O-Meter ceased, and the tapping got louder. It sounded like footsteps, almost as if someone was running through the attic. Holly heard a key turning, followed by a creaking similar to that of an old door hinge. A loud bang echoed, as though a door had been slammed shut. There was a moment of silence. Holly could feel her heart beating like a drum.

Suddenly, she heard muffled grunting. Holly ran down the attic staircase to the door that separated the attic from the mansion. She stopped halfway down the stairs when a pounding began accompanying the grunting. Holly scanned the shelves along the staircase that were stuffed with paint cans to find the source of the noise. Then she looked up to the ceiling. Her gaze lingered there.

Was that a door in the ceiling above the staircase? It looked like it had been painted over with the same granite color as the rest of the ceiling and was so well camouflaged that Holly hadn't ever noticed it before.

She scampered back to the top of the staircase and stood on her toes to scan the top of the shelves. She spotted a dust-covered stick with a hook attached to its end and reached out to grab it. She carefully threaded the hook through the metal ring on the ceiling door and pulled with all her might.

With a squeak, a staircase unfolded down to Holly's feet. Her heart beat in time with the muffled grunts above.

"It's pigeons, just pigeons," she mumbled, trying to convince herself that everything was under control. She took a deep breath and climbed the stairs.

The musty smell of mold and dust tickled her nose as she peeked into a secret room. It was filled to the brim with boxes and old furniture. In the center of the room, dimly lit by the sunbeams falling through the attic windows high above the rafters, was a rectangular shape covered with a dirty cloth. The grunting sound seemed to be coming from there. Holly's body shook with fear so terribly that she began to feel her legs weakening. She slowly sat on the floor. Common sense was telling her to leave but her curiosity kept her there.

"W-w-who's there?" she stuttered, crawling on all fours toward the sound. Then, plucking up all her courage, she darted forward and whisked off the dirty cloth. The grunting stopped.

She saw a massive wooden chest covered with elaborate carvings. The front panel was decorated with an image of an island. Holly traced the image with her finger. The same animals that were embossed in the coat of arms on the encyclopedia soared over the landscape. People with cone-shaped heads strolled among butterflies through the narrow alleys of the town. A gigantic castle towered above all and over that, an embedded silver plate read, "Magora."

"Magora," she said surprised. "Just like the encyclopedia."

Hammering from inside the chest interrupted her thoughts. A loud grunt followed and Holly jumped back. Her forgotten fear crawled up into her throat again, and she felt as if two hands were trying to strangle her. She breathed heavily. Unable to resist her curiosity, she stretched out her right hand, turned the heavy iron key, and leaped back to the folding staircase. She waited there, ready to escape from whatever might come out of the chest.

The grunting stopped, followed by seconds of complete silence. Then, the lid of the chest slowly creaked open. Holly gaped with astonishment at two tiny paws covered with fluffy orange fur. Behind the paws, two frightened green eyes appeared. What followed looked like an orange koala with a humanoid face, like that of a child. It had pointy ears and short arms and legs.

"How in the world?" Holly rubbed her eyes. "It's a Nukimai."

Grandpa Nikolas had painted creatures he told her were called Nukimais many times, but Holly had always thought he had made them up. She pinched her arm to see if she was awake, but the Nukimai did not vanish. Instead, it grunted, wiggled its long, pointy ears, and with a thump, bounced to the floor. It curled up into a ball like an armadillo and rolled right to Holly's feet.

Holly laughed when she saw the fuzzy ball. Her fears vanished in an instant.

She leaned down and read, "Tenshi" on its collar. "Wait a minute." Holly pulled the letter from her pocket and read, "'Take good care of Tenshi.'"

Magora, Tenshi, the letter, the cloaked creature—they must be all connected somehow. But where had this creature come from? Where was this land of Magora? And what role did she play in all of this?

"Do you know where Magora is?" Holly asked Tenshi.

He wrinkled his silky black muzzle, ruffled his orange fur, and grunted loudly. His bright-green eyes widened as someone shouted from the mansion below.

"Holly! We have to tell you something."

"The Smoralls are coming," Holly gasped.

She picked up Tenshi and climbed down the ladder. With a click, she closed the hidden attic door above her and stuffed the little critter under her sweater. "Be quiet now, or we'll be in big trouble," Holly admonished.

With a loud bang, the door to Holly's attic room flung open.

THE GALLERY OF WONDERS

The Hidden Attic

The struggle to balance fantasy and reality is part of learning that the two can't exist without each other. Reality is fantasy and fantasy is reality. It all depends on the viewpoint. And the line becomes unimportant.

Ms. Smorall and Barb came into the attic and dropped a bucket and a broom at Holly's feet.

"We are headed out to Nikolas' funeral right now," said Ms. Smorall. "We have to host a gathering afterward. Then we can meet with the lawyer and collect the inheritance."

"Can't I come to the funeral?" Holly asked.

"Are you kidding?" said Barb. "Who is going to sweep the floors and clean the bathrooms? Do you think they'll clean themselves?"

"By the time we get back, I want everything to be sparkling clean for the gathering, and for you to be back up in the attic," said Ms. Smorall. "Don't even think about coming downstairs while the mourners are here. The last thing we need is sniveling child like you."

Holly's heart sank. She wouldn't even be allowed to say goodbye to her grandfather.

All day long Holly scrubbed the floors, her eyes overflowing with tears. Her only thoughts were of Grandpa Nikolas and how much she was going to miss him. Not even Tenshi and all the magical objects she had found in the package could cheer her up.

Just as she was crawling on her knees along the hallway, polishing every inch of the fine marble floor, a dark, raspy voice echoed through the mansion. It sounded eerie.

"Holly, where are you?"

Holly jumped up from the floor. Her heart was racing like a bullet train. Where was the voice coming from? She looked around but didn't see anything. Still, she wondered if maybe it was the cloaked creature she had seen at the fire. Had it followed her here? Shaking, she held her breath and listened.

The voice echoed again. "Holly. Holly."

Was someone really calling her name? Holly pressed her hands against her ears and shook her head. The voice stopped and Holly continued polishing the marble. She had probably just imagined it.

In the afternoon, the Smoralls returned and the mourners began to arrive. An unmistakable screechy voice echoed in the hallway.

"Urgh, Hubbleworth," Holly muttered, tiptoeing down the stairs to sneak a peek.

Thankfully, Ms. Hubbleworth had realized that pink was too bright and flashy for a funeral. She arrived drenched in purple from head to toe. Unfortunately, the rest of the wardrobe wasn't much of an improvement. She wore an extremely long violet velvet cloak with black frills over a dark purple dress decorated with lace and pearls. Her blonde beehive was topped with a huge hat with flowers on top of it. From her arm dangled a purple handbag with black dots.

"Jeepers," Holly said, repulsed by the fashion disaster. How could anyone have such a lack of taste?

Ms. Hubbleworth crossed the marble hallway to make her appearance in the living room, dragging an endless train of velvet behind her.

Holly peeked around the corner into the living room to find it filled with mourners. The atmosphere was stifling.

Rufus was standing by the buffet table.

"Rufus, come here," Holly whispered.

Rufus winked at her and snuck out of the living room.

"You won't believe what has happened," Holly said. "I have to tell you all about it."

"What is it?" Rufus asked.

"You go get Brian," ordered Holly. "I'll wait in the billiard room."

Holly ran back to the attic and placed Tenshi inside her backpack, motioning for him to be quiet. Then she went to the billiard room.

"What is going on?" asked Brian when he came into the

room with Rufus.

"Trust me. It's very important," Holly said, placing the backpack on the billiard table and untying the top.

A grunt came from the bag. Brian looked curiously at the backpack. An orange paw appeared, followed by Tenshi's big, round eyes.

"Holy smokes, what on earth is that?" Brian pushed his glasses up on the bridge of his nose.

"It's a Nukimai," said Holly. "His name is Tenshi."

"You mean one of those creatures your grandfather used to paint?" Brian asked. "They're real?"

Holly nodded. She told her friends the whole story and even demonstrated the Shrink-O-Meter on the little jar with the smelly powder.

"Wow." That was all Brian could say after Holly had finished her story.

"Do you have any idea who sent you these things?" asked Rufus, eyeing the *Encyclopedia of Magora*. "They are extraordinary."

"I thought you might be able to give me an answer," said Holly. "You're the brainy one."

"At present, we do not have any clues that could lead us to any conclusions," said Rufus. "We would have to examine the chest again and study these objects in detail."

"Wow," said Brian, still stunned.

"Can you say anything but wow?" asked Holly, while shrinking the encyclopedia to miniature size.

"Yes, this is incredible. Wow." Brian stared at Tenshi with his mouth wide open.

"Quiet," Rufus whispered, putting his finger to his lips. "What was that?"

There was a sound coming from the hallway.

"I can hear it, too," Holly said, leaping to the door and pulling it open. A white poodle shot into the room.

"Come back, Chi-Chi," echoed a voice through the hallway.

A moment later, a young girl with long blonde hair and big blue eyes appeared in the doorframe.

"Amanda? What are you doing here?" Holly asked, annoyed to see the girl she hated the most in school.

"So we meet again, Scribble Queen," said Amanda, laughing.

"What are you doing here?" Holly repeated.

"Well—I was—you know—" stammered Amanda. She straightened her elegant black dress.

"You were what?" Brian asked.

"I had to go to the bathroom," Amanda said. "But then I heard voices, and so—"

"So you just eavesdropped," Brian interrupted.

"Great. Now we're stuck with her," Holly said.

"You overheard our whole conversation?" Rufus asked.

"Of course I heard you, little goofball," said Amanda. "I would also like to know if there's anything else in that chest. We really should go up to the attic." She picked up her poodle and went back into the hallway.

Holly ground her teeth. She was so angry she could have dragged Amanda out of the room and locked her in the bathroom. Everything about Amanda repulsed her. She was arrogant, gossipy, and only cared about her looks. Most of all, she was an extremely good painter. That just made matters worse. But Holly realized that locking her up wouldn't solve the problem.

"Come on," said Amanda, glancing back over her shoulder. "We'd better find out more about that chest."

Rufus lifted his eyebrows and sighed. "I believe she is trying to imply that she will join us from here on."

"You're a smart little goofball," said Amanda. "Maybe there is a magic wand in the chest that can get me a new curling iron." She grinned at Holly. "By the way, what would Ms. Smorall say if she heard she has an alien orange critter in her house?"

"This is considered blackmail," Rufus said to Holly. "She is saying that if we do not integrate her into our plans, she will take certain measures."

"I know what she's saying," said Holly, annoyed at Rufus repeatedly stating the obvious. "Can't you just say anything simply and plainly for once?"

"Come on," Amanda commanded as she led the group through the hallway.

Brian whispered into Holly's ear, "I'll gag her."

"Be my guest," Holly said as she pushed past Amanda and walked up the marble staircase.

Once in front of the attic door, Holly stopped. "I need a few minutes," she said. "This is my room, and I want to clean up a few things before people come in."

Her real intention was to get to the chest and remove anything important so that Amanda couldn't get hold of it.

"Okay, but hurry up," Amanda said.

Holly went into the attic and closed the door behind her. Once she had pulled down the ladder above the staircase, she climbed up to the hidden room and opened the chest again. Inside were a mahogany case and a neatly-folded piece of canvas. A grunt came from her backpack, and Tenshi bounced out, right into the chest. He grabbed the mahogany case, held it up, and tapped on the lid. Holly flipped it open. Inside was a thin, golden paintbrush with an intricately carved handle, lying on a purple silk cushion.

On the underside of the lid was a golden plate with an engraving that read:

The Magic Brush

Holly took the paintbrush out of the case. Underneath, she found a piece of parchment. It read:

Instructions: 1. Draw three circles in the air. 2. Create the image of a gate in your mind. 3. A gate will open.

"What gate?" Holly asked Tenshi. "And what is this?" She picked up the folded canvas and moved a few boxes aside. She then spread the canvas on the floor. A marvelous painting lay in front of her. She was overwhelmed by the details of a bustling medieval town surrounding a towering castle. It showed the same town that had been carved into the chest. Ornate letters above the painting read "Magora." At the bottom was Nikolas O'Flanigan's signature.

"So that's what Magora is, a fantasy painting Grandpa

Nikolas created," Holly said.

Tenshi grunted as if he had understood what she had said.

Holly glanced at the magic brush again and wondered if she should try it.

She read the instructions again, waved the brush three times, and focused on an image of a gate she had seen in one of Grandpa Nikolas' paintings. Bright sparkles shot from the brush onto the canvas. Tenshi rolled behind the oak chest. Holly dropped the brush and stumbled back as a loud humming filled the air. She leaped over a few boxes and hid behind them.

The sparkles hovered a foot above the painting and turned into a veil of mist, which spun like a miniature tornado. The painting disappeared. The floor opened up and bright light burst from it. The humming stopped. A shining lake of lights lay in front of Holly.

"What on earth is that?" asked a voice.

Holly whirled around. Amanda stood in the attic, her eyes wide open, pointing at the gate of lights. Brian and Rufus were standing next to her. Before Holly could say a word, Amanda's poodle sped toward Tenshi, barking ferociously. Amanda held onto the leash, stumbled forward, lost balance, and fell right into the shining lake, making a sound like a large bubble bursting.

Suddenly, Amanda and her poodle were gone.

The Gate

The line between fantasy and reality can be either vibrant or dull. It all depends on the color you paint it.

Tenshi curled up and rolled toward the lights on the floor.

"Watch it!" Holly shouted to Brian. "Tenshi is heading for the hole, too."

"No!" yelled Brian. He leaped forward, stumbled over a box, and both of them fell into the lake. At the sound of two more bubbles bursting, Brian and Tenshi disappeared.

Frozen in place, Holly stared at Rufus. She could feel sweat running down her face.

"What now?" Rufus asked.

Holly couldn't move. She was terrified inside but didn't dare show it. Rufus was scared too. Frightening him even more was the last thing she wanted to do.

"We have to help Brian," she said.

"Oh no, we are not doing this," Rufus said, shaking his head back and forth anxiously. "We do not even know where it leads."

Holly knew that she had to go after Brian, with or without Rufus. "If you don't come, I will go alone." Holly stepped to the edge of the gate.

"You are not going to leave me here all by myself," said Rufus. "How am I going to explain this to everyone?"

"That's your problem," said Holly, ready to jump.

"All right, all right, I will come with you." Rufus grabbed Holly's hand.

"Ready?" Holly asked.

Rufus nodded reluctantly.

They stepped into what had been the painting a few moments earlier, dropped a few feet, and shot down a tunnel of fog.

"Watch out, Rufus!" Holly screamed. She tried to hold on to something, but there was nothing but millions of lights that zoomed past her like fireflies. She glanced back over her shoulder. Rufus glided awkwardly in zigzag lines behind her, pressing his hands over his eyes.

"There's the end in front of us," yelled Holly. She dropped like a boulder from a height of about five feet.

Holly fell out of the air, right onto Amanda's leg. She yelped.

"Out of the way. Rufus is coming," said Holly, pushing Amanda to the side.

That same second, Rufus' scream filled the air above, and

with an unceremonious thump, he hit the ground next to Holly.

"This was a b-b-bad idea," he stuttered.

"Where the heck is Chi-Chi?" Amanda asked.

"Nobody cares about your stupid poodle," Brian said, rubbing his elbow. "I'd rather know where we are."

They had landed in a lush meadow full of green-spotted orchids.

Holly grabbed Tenshi by his pointy ears and shoved him back into her backpack. "You are not going to run away a second time," she said.

Tenshi growled briefly but did not resist.

A grassy hill was in front of them. Intrigued, Holly climbed it. She gasped in astonishment when she reached the top. Never had she seen such a spectacular view.

"What is it? Where are we?" Amanda asked, stomping up the hill.

Holly's eyes wandered over the landscape below. A turquoise lake surrounded an island overcrowded with crooked buildings. They were built in Tudor-style, half stucco and half pieces of dark wood with small, diamond-paned windows. An ancient castle towered above them all. It was the kind of castle Holly had only heard about in fairytales. The houses were nestled right up against the gigantic walls of the castle. Many slender turrets were connected by bridges, which Holly couldn't even begin to count. The sunlight draped the magical city with a soft, ochre light.

"Amazing," said Holly. "This is Magora. It is Grandpa Nikolas' painting."

"Great!" Amanda said. "Is that supposed to mean we're stuck in a painting?"

Brian and Rufus followed them up the hill.

"Due to the fall, we must be experiencing some kind of hallucination," Rufus said.

Amanda pinched Rufus' arm.

Rufus let out a yowl. "What did you do that for?" he asked.

"Did that feel like a hallucination, you nerd?" Amanda asked.

On a mountain range in the distance, towering on the highest peak, Holly could barely make out the ruin of another castle. Black clouds that seemed permanently attached to the rundown turrets surrounded the ruin. Holly's heart pounded rapidly. She didn't understand why, but somehow she felt her future was inextricably linked to that castle.

Holly heard a familiar scream behind her. She spun around.

"Ms. Hubbleworth?" she said, astonished.

Holly's nosy next-door neighbor climbed out of a ditch. Her garish sunhat dangled on a ribbon around her neck, and her dress was covered in mud. She flicked a slimy worm from her eyebrows and screamed so loudly that the butterflies in the meadow shot away into the distance.

She tried to wipe the mud off her dress. "Where am I?" She demanded.

"What are you doing here?" Holly asked.

"The dog barked, and I heard all that noise upstairs, so I went up to the attic," said Ms. Hubbleworth. "The next thing I

remember, I tripped over my dress, zoomed down a tunnel of lights, and landed in that smelly ditch."

Ms. Hubbleworth snorted like a horse while marching up the hill. When she reached the top, her mouth dropped open.

"What is this place?" she asked. "If you don't send me back right now I will—" She stopped, leaped forward, and grabbed Holly by the ear. "I want to go back to Donkleywood. Now!"

"Maybe we can climb back up the tunnel," Holly suggested, standing on her tiptoes to try to ease the yanking on her ear. She glanced back to where the gate had been. But to her surprise, there was nothing. The opening in the sky had closed. Ms. Hubbleworth pulled Holly further onto her toes.

A soothing but admonishing voice echoed from the bottom of the hill. "Joline Hubbleworth, keep yourself under control."

A woman with long black hair had appeared in the meadow. Even though she was over seven feet tall, she appeared fragile because of her thinness. Her arms were thin as sticks, and her long neck reached high up like that of a gazelle. A white silken dress contrasted with her black hair that reached all the way down to her knees. Her facial features were Asian, and her skull was oddly-shaped. From a distance, it looked as if a flower was actually growing from the woman's head. But at second glance, Holly realized that the blossom was made of bone and was part of the woman's skull. Butterflies of all colors and sizes fluttered around the bony flower, entering and leaving the woman's head.

"Professor Hubbleworth, you really should know better," the woman admonished mildly.

"*P-p-professor* Hubbleworth?" Ms. Hubbleworth squeezed her eyes shut and released Holly's ear. "No, no, I'm dreaming. I'm dreaming."

"The woman with that flower on her head looks so real," Brian whispered into Holly's ear. "If Grandpa Nikolas painted her, he did an amazing job."

"Excuse me, ma'am. May I ask who you are?" Holly asked.

"I'm Professor Leguthiandra LePawnee," said the woman. "Please follow me." She turned to the muttering Ms. Hubbleworth. "Joline, would you please stop this nonsense? I didn't even notice that you had left the Academy."

"The Academy?" Ms. Hubbleworth screeched as if she were about to be beheaded. She opened her eyes and stared at the tall woman. "An academy? You mean a school? With children?"

"Come. Follow me," Professor LePawnee said. "Everything is all right."

Holly felt that nothing was really all right. She had no clue where they were and why Ms. Hubbleworth was a professor. A professor of what?

They strolled down through the meadow in silence and reached the turquoise lake. Professor LePawnee pulled out a paintbrush from the sleeve of her silken dress.

"This is Lake Santima," the professor said. "We'll be in Magora shortly."

At least Holly now knew that this really was the Magora painting they were in. She still wondered where they were headed.

Professor LePawnee lifted the brush high above her head, drew something in the air, and focused on the brush. Sparks shot out from the tip. As if squeezed out of a tube, paint spattered from the brush into the air and whirled around like a tornado. In the center of the tornado, an object materialized.

"Jeepers," Holly cried out. "That looks like some kind of ship."

The paint solidified, and a solid boat that could fit at least ten people landed in front of them. Professor LePawnee clapped her hands. From the distance came a creature flying through the air toward them.

"That looks like a lion," Amanda said.

"No, it's a giant bird," Brian corrected.

The creature became clearer as it approached.

"It is a griffin," explained Rufus. "Griffins are eagles with the body of a lion."

A silver-gray eight-foot-tall griffin landed in front of the boat and squawked at them. Professor LePawnee attached the reins of the boat to it and said, "Let's go before Cuspidor notices we are in his territory."

Holly knew she had heard the name Cuspidor somewhere before. It irritated her, but she didn't know why. She tried to remember where she had heard it, but she couldn't place it. She sat down on one of the wooden benches in the bow of the boat.

Ms. Hubbleworth made herself comfortable in the stern, as far away from Holly as possible. The griffin spread his wings and whizzed up into the air. The boat jerked and a moment later, they were being pulled across Lake Santima.

Holly leaned over the side of the boat and looked ahead. Three crystal domes, each one larger than any dome she had ever seen, appeared in the distance. They were peeking out of the lake as if a cathedral had been flooded and only the domes were now visible. The blue-tinted glass didn't seem to hold water inside.

"What are they?" Holly asked.

"These are glass domes on top of a few caverns," said Professor LePawnee. "Many years ago they were used for storage, but we have closed them because they were unsound. It was also too dangerous because of Cuspidor."

There was that name again. It was time Holly found out who this person was. She turned to the professor. "Who is Cuspidor?" she asked.

LePawnee nervously twiddled her hair between her fingers. She moved closer to Holly. With her hand half-covering her mouth, she whispered, "His real name is S.A. Lokin. He is the Duke of Cuspidor."

Nobody could really overhear them in the middle of the lake, but the professor acted as if there were spies all around.

"He wants to destroy Magora." She pointed to the ruin of the castle on the mountain range. "He lives in the mountains of the land of Cuspidor."

"Why does he want to destroy Magora?" Rufus asked.

"It's a long story."

Rufus pulled a notebook from his coat. Holly knew he had gotten into the habit of jotting things down that might be of use.

"We have plenty of time," said Rufus. "Let us begin."

Gindars

When you paint the line in bright colors, it becomes very strong, so strong that it takes the focus off reality and fantasy.

Professor LePawnee nodded and began her story. "Legend has it that a long time ago, Magora was created by a powerful Gindar—"

Surprised, Holly jumped up. "Gindar?" she said. The boat rocked to one side and almost flipped over. She remembered the box with all the mysterious objects that was addressed to "Gindar Holly O'Flanigan."

"Watch it!" Amanda yelled. "Do you want to drown us?"

Holly sat back down on the bench.

"What is a Gindar?" Holly asked.

"A Gindar is a highly-talented painter," Professor LePawnee

explained.

Holly could not believe what she was hearing. Was she a gifted painter? All her life she had been told she had no talent.

"Gindars are very rare, but Magora depends on their creativity. They can paint anything they like and make it come alive. If it wasn't for their talent, Magora wouldn't exist—"

"Do you have a mirror?" Amanda interrupted. She didn't seem particularly interested in the topic. "My makeup must be a mess, and my hair feels like straw," she complained.

"Amanda, would you shut up?" said Brian. "We're discussing important issues here."

"No, I don't have a mirror," replied Professor LePawnee. "Ledesmas don't use mirrors."

"What is a Ledesma?" Amanda asked.

Holly jumped up again. "Now wait, Amanda. One thing at a time. First, let me get something straight. Gindars are painters who paint what other people can't, right?"

"Correct," Professor LePawnee said.

"Then you must be a Gindar because you made this boat become real," Holly said.

"No." the professor smiled, almost embarrassed. "I'm not. Gindars can create living beings, and I can't do that."

A swarm of fingernail-sized butterflies fluttered from the woman's bony flower into the sky, whirled around like a tornado, and disappeared in the clouds. A few seconds later, a new batch of butterflies shot down from the sky and swooped back into her head.

Holly wondered what those butterflies were doing in the

woman's head, but she thought it might be rude to ask.

"Let me explain," said Professor LePawnee. "In Magora, life is centered around painting. There are three types of painters. First, there are Gindars. Gindars are highly-gifted people who can create anything they want, but they focus on painting people and animals. The second type of painter is a Legumer. Legumers are like Gindars, but they can only create plants and objects. Tracers are the third group. They copy everything except living beings. Each Tracer specializes in a certain field, and they provide Magora with a steady supply of food and goods. Gindars and Legumers have the power to create new things, but a Tracer can only make copies. Each painter has a paintbrush with special powers that allows him to create these things—just as I have created this boat."

Holly peeked over Rufus' shoulder into his notebook. He had written down every word Professor LePawnee had said.

"Gindar, Legumer, Tracer," Holly read out loud.

The classification of painters was similar to that which Grandpa Nikolas had told her some time ago, although he had called them true artists, creative artists, and technical artists.

Holly didn't understand why she would get a letter addressed to "Gindar Holly O'Flanigan." She was not gifted—at least that was what everybody always told her.

"If someone is a Gindar, he would know of his talent, wouldn't he?" she asked.

"Not necessarily," said Professor LePawnee. "Gindars need training, just as any other painter does. They are like unpolished diamonds that must be refined. In essence, that is what we do at Cliffony."

"Cliffo-what?" Brian asked.

"Cliffony Academy of the Arts," answered Professor LePawnee, pointing at the majestic castle on the island. "Cliffony is at the center of Magora. This is where we train new painters."

Fairytale-like buildings nestled like toys against the massive outer wall of Cliffony. A dozen turrets towered over the gigantic entrance gate. On each turret, a flag billowed with Cliffony's coat of arms depicting two griffins wrapped around a paintbrush. Holly remembered the coat of arm from the cover of the encyclopedia.

"Now I want to know what a Ledesma is," Amanda demanded.

"Ledesmas are creations of one of the greatest Gindars of all time," said Professor LePawnee. "The butterflies in our heads are our minds. We are in constant communication with other Ledesmas through these butterflies. Every Ledesma can find out what the other is doing. We can look into each other's minds."

"If you know everything about each other, then you don't have any privacy," Holly said.

"Correct. But we don't mind," said Professor LePawnee. "We see it as an asset to our species. We can learn much more by working together rather than isolating ourselves."

"Aren't there any Ledesmas who want privacy?" Holly asked.

A batch of butterflies approached. Holly observed them carefully. After all the research she had done for her biology class, she felt like an expert on them. These butterflies, however,

had six wings instead of four and fluttered much faster than regular butterflies.

"Having privacy is an odd concept to us—" LePawnee hesitated. "Well, there has been one case—but that was unusual."

"What case?" Rufus pressed.

"There was a Ledesma who went by the name of Butterfly," the professor answered reluctantly. "She went on a journey to research a tribe in Asia. Upon her return, Butterfly was no longer willing to share her knowledge."

"What happened to her?" Holly asked.

Nervously, LePawnee looked around, moved a bit closer, and whispered behind her hand. "She's dead."

"She is what?" Rufus asked.

"You heard her, goofball," said Amanda. "She's dead. Now let's talk about something more pleasant. Do you have beauty parlors in Magora?"

"Amanda." Brian rolled his eyes and slapped his forehead.

Holly wanted to ask LePawnee what had happened to Butterfly, but from the Ledesma's expression, she gathered that it was probably not a good idea. Obviously, something had happened that the professor didn't feel comfortable talking about.

As they approached Magora, the sky filled with griffins. In their midst were also a few prehistoric flying dinosaurs, each with four wings and a giraffe-like neck.

"The Department of Transportation has now regulated air travel only to griffins," said LePawnee. "Some people still use dinosaurs, but they should be pulled out of traffic in the next four years. Anyway, all you have to concern yourself with right now is the exam next week."

"Exam?" Holly and Brian bellowed at the same time. That word implied studying, and Holly didn't like that idea too much.

Rufus, on the other hand, seemed quite excited. He flipped open his notebook. "What kind of test will we be having?" he asked.

"Your entry exam to Cliffony," LePawnee said.

"I don't like tests," Holly said.

"You had better get used to them," said LePawnee. "Next year, you will have to take another one, for the Quadrennial Art Competition."

"What is that?" Rufus asked.

"You will find out soon enough," said the professor.

"You must be kidding," said Holly. "We are not going to school here."

"Holly is right," said Rufus. "We have to find a way to get back home. We cannot stay here."

"I'm certainly not staying," muttered Ms. Hubbleworth from the rear of the boat. "Take me back now."

Professor LePawnee directed the griffin around a cliff to a beach and docked the boat gently on the shore. Everybody climbed out of the boat except Ms. Hubbleworth.

"I'm not going anywhere," she snapped. "I'm too old to take an exam."

"Joline, what's wrong with you today?" said LePawnee, sighing. "Of course you will not take an exam. The children will."

"I'm so relieved," Ms. Hubbleworth said as she climbed out of the boat.

The professor waved her brush and focused on the tip. Sparks shot out and encircled the boat. Like a watercolor painting in the rain, the boat dissolved instantly. The paint slipped back into the tip of the brush, and every trace of it vanished. The griffin flew off into the distance.

"Let's go now," LePawnee said. "We still have to pass the Gors."

They followed her. Holly wondered who or what the Gors were, but the professor did not say a word. Instead, she led them up to the top of one of the dunes.

When they reached the peak, Brian hollered, "Holy smokes. Those must be the Gors."

Holly stepped up behind Brian and looked down the dune. Her stomach turned.

THE GALLERY OF WONDERS

The Wall of Gors

Dull colors can make the line very subtle. Strong colors allow it to stick out and give fantasy and reality stronger contrast.

Below them were hundreds of giant boar-like creatures. Their long tusks crossed in front of their snouts, linking each Gor to the next in line. They stood on their hind feet frozen like statues, dressed in rusted armor, forming a living wall around the perimeter of Magora. Holding sharp swords in their clawed paws, they kept their eyes closed. The stench of rotten flesh filled the air. Holly pulled her sweater up over her nose.

"The Gors will drain your mind and leave your body empty though still alive," said Le Pawnee. "Just as vultures sense carrion, Gors detect minds and destroy them. Watch this."

She pointed at a pigeon that was approaching the Gors. The professor threw a few sunflower seeds at the Gors' claws. The pigeon fluttered over and started picking at them. The earth shook, and suddenly the Gors opened their eyes. Their pupils flickered as if they were made of glowing lava. A crimson light shot from their eyes, knocking the pigeon to the ground with a thud. There was silence for a split second. Then the pigeon shook violently and rays of light blasted out of every inch of its head. The Gors sucked up the light with their eyes and then closed them. Silence fell over the scene.

"The pigeon looks dead somehow, even though it is still standing," Holly whispered.

"Its mind *is* dead," LePawnee said.

Suddenly, the pigeon trotted straight ahead.

"Its body doesn't know what to do anymore because there is no mind to control it," said LePawnee. "Only very basic functions remain, like walking and breathing and some fundamental instinctive behaviors."

"How are we ever going to pass the Gors?" Rufus asked as he stared in clear panic at the pigeon.

"Separate mind from body, then split your mind, and then you will enter. Stay whole, and you will die," LePawnee said.

"What are you talking about?" Brian asked.

"It's more important that my nails don't get split," said Amanda as she polished her fingernails.

"How can you think about your nails at a time like this?" Brian asked.

"This is just a fake world we're in," said Amanda. "Why worry? A painting can't do us any harm."

"Amanda is right," said Holly. "All of this comes from Grandpa Nikolas' imagination. Imagination can't cause physical harm."

"Yes, it can," LePawnee said. "Once you have entered a painting, you become part of it. Then anything you see or do becomes real."

"That changes things, doesn't it, Goldilocks?" Brian said.

Amanda stopped polishing her nails. Her expression changed from disdain to fear.

"We will pass the Gors now," said the professor. She searched her pockets. "Oh no, I forgot the MSP. I will go and get some. You stay here and wait for me."

LePawnee closed her eyes before Holly could ask her what MSP was. Like a jet of water spouting from a fountain, Ledesma butterflies shot out of the professor's head. They scattered in all directions, soared high into the sky, and fluttered across the Wall of Gors.

"Professor LePawnee? Are you all right?" asked Holly.

The professor's eyes were closed. With abrupt movements, she marched toward the Gors.

"Don't. They'll hurt you!" Holly yelled and tried to pull her back by the sleeve.

But LePawnee was too strong and kept walking until she passed the Gors. Not once did she open her eyes. A second later, the professor disappeared behind a dune.

Horror-struck, Holly glanced at Brian. She was speechless.

Rufus broke the silence. "What did she mean by MSP?"

Holly shook her head. She didn't really understand what had just happened.

"I think we should try to pass the Gors ourselves," Brian said. "She might have left us here for a reason. I don't know if we can trust her."

"Professor LePawnee told us to wait here," said Rufus. "Forget it. I am not going through that wall. I trust her."

"You're such a chicken," Brian said.

"No, I am not," Rufus said.

"I think LePawnee gave us a hint," Holly interrupted. "She told us that we have to separate our minds from our bodies and split it into pieces. The Gors want minds, not bodies."

"And how are we supposed to do that?" Amanda asked as she sat down on a rock and began straightening her bangs.

"Dunno." Holly shrugged, discouraged. She trudged to a sand dune close by and dropped like a stone onto her backpack. Her backpack made a grunt.

"Jeepers! I completely forgot about Tenshi." Holly untied her backpack, and Tenshi wobbled out, holding the miniature *Encyclopedia of Magora* in his paws.

"I totally forgot the encyclopedia," said Holly, excitedly. "We might find something about the Gors in here." She un-shrunk the encyclopedia with the Shrink-O-Meter.

When she saw the book, she remembered where she had heard about Cuspidor.

"Listen," Holly said. "It says here on the back cover, 'The volume includes a special section on the creation of Ledesmas and the battle against S.A. Lokin, Duke of Cuspidor.'"

"But that doesn't get us anywhere," Brian said.

Holly noticed that Rufus' eyes began to sparkle. She knew that anytime her friend saw a new book, his adrenaline level

skyrocketed. Holly dropped the weighty volume into Rufus' arms.

"Here, take it," she said. "I'm not going to read this. You can make better use of it."

"Thank you," said Rufus. "The old paper and the leather smell so good." He ran his face over the cover as if he wanted to kiss the book. Then he put it under his arm and walked behind a sand dune. "I will read a bit until Professor LePawnee comes back."

"What a nerd," said Brian. "He's way too brainy for his age."

Holly nodded as she emptied the contents of her backpack. She sat cross-legged in front of the pile of objects and un-shrunk them one by one.

Ms. Hubbleworth cursed at Holly from a dune above. "You got me into all of this. If you don't get me out of this place, I will report to the police that you have kidnapped me—provided there is something like that on such an island."

"She's a nightmare," said Brian, picking up the powder-filled jar from the pile of objects. "I wonder what this is for."

Holly snatched the jar from him. "Wait a second. That's it," she said, shaking the jar. "MSP, short for Mind-Splitting Powder. That's what Professor LePawnee said she was going to get."

She turned the jar around and read the label.

"Bingo. Listen to this," Holly said excitedly. "'Instructions for passing the Wall of Gors. Sprinkle a fingertip of Mind-Splitting Powder over your head and—'"

Holly wasn't able to finish her sentence. Ms. Hubbleworth

briskly leaped down the dune, grabbed the jar from Holly, and popped the cork open. "I'm not going to stay here with a bunch of children. Let me try that," she said. She sprinkled the white powder over her beehive. Her face froze as she dropped the jar. Rays of light shot out of her body and into the sky. Emotionless, like a puppet on a string, she walked straight toward the Gors, just as the pigeon had done.

"Jeepers," cried Holly as she jumped up. She picked up the jar and glanced over the instructions. "I hope she read the rest—it says you have to concentrate on reuniting your mind with your body on the other side of the Wall of Gors. If you don't do that, your mind will enter the object you last concentrated on."

"I'm sure her mind will get stuck in a cactus. Thorns fit her nature," Brian snickered.

Holly watched as Ms. Hubbleworth passed the Gors and vanished into the distance.

"Let's try it," said Holly. "If we follow the instructions carefully, it should work."

"Rufus?" Brian hollered over the dune. "Come over here. We found a way in."

Rufus appeared from behind the sand dune, balancing the encyclopedia in his left hand while running his right index finger over the ornate lettering on the parchment.

"Listen to this," he said. "'Legends place the origin of the powerful Gindar S.A. Lokin in another world but, so far, there is no scientific proof of it. Lokin, also known as Cuspidor, was able to unite the evil forces against the island of Magora. He conquered the mainland around Lake Santima and established

his empire in the mountains of Cuspidor."

Rufus flipped a few pages. "He has tried several times to overthrow Magora until the last powerful Gindar, the Wise Man, created the Wall of Gors around the island and stopped any further incursion. Since the disappearance of the Wise Man, the Gors have ensured the survival of Magora. It is advised by the High Council to remain within the borders of the wall. Anyone outside could be in great peril.'" Rufus slammed the encyclopedia shut and tucked it under his arm.

"Then we'd better get out of here right now," Brian said.

Holly nodded. She began to read out the MSP instructions, "'Sprinkle a fingertip of Mind-Splitting Powder over your head. Concentrate on reuniting your mind with your body on the other side of the Wall of Gors.'"

Holly gave everyone some MSP and sprinkled a little over Tenshi's head. Within a split second, lights shot out of everyone's head.

Brian and Rufus marched like zombies toward the Gors. Amanda and Tenshi followed. Holly shrunk the objects, packed them up, and was about to sprinkle some MSP over her head when she heard a deep, raspy voice call her name. It reverberated in her head as if echoing in an empty castle. She whirled, but there was nobody in sight.

"Holly, where are you?" the voice boomed.

Horrified, Holly spun in a circle. It was the same voice she had heard in the marble hallway of the Smoralls' mansion. But this time, Holly knew it was not her imagination. The voice sounded very clear and dangerous.

Holly shuddered and felt she had to get away quickly. She

sprinkled some MSP over her hair.

A humming noise began in her head. Her vision faded. She felt pressure inside her skull and a force pounding against her scalp. There was a loud crack as if her skull had burst open. She was comforted by a sudden sense of freedom and lightness, as if she were being carried away on a fluffy cloud into the sky. Never before had she felt so tranquil and free. When her vision came back, she realized that she was hovering in the air. Below, she saw her body marching toward the Gors.

"Split your mind," she said, trying not to get distracted by the stunning view of Magora. "Split your mind." Suddenly, her mind was everywhere. She could look at Magora from dozens of angles at the same time. "It's working," she said, relieved.

Like a swarm of thoughts, her mind flew over the Wall of Gors, while her empty body marched below. "Now, concentrate on your body," she said. Once again, she lost her vision, and she felt pain as if a hammer had dropped on her skull. She heard a loud whack and all the tranquility and freedom were gone.

Holly felt as if she were trapped inside a dark room with no escape. She felt sick, and a moment later, she fainted.

The Trip to the Hatchery

Balancing the colors of the line is like walking on a tightrope. You don't want the rope to be the center of attention, but the acrobat.

$\mathscr{A}$ soothing voice reverberated in Holly's mind. "Are you all right?"

The fuzzy outline of an old man's face became visible. His long white hair was neatly combed back, and his bushy eyebrows hung over a pair of reading glasses.

Looking worried, Professor LePawnee peered over the man's shoulder. "Gerald, I'm sorry. I shouldn't have left them alone," she said.

"Don't worry, Leguthiandra. They'll be fine," replied the man, swinging a paintbrush like a pendulum over Holly's face. "It takes a while for the mind to reenter the body. It's surprising how well they handled the MSP. Their minds could have gotten stuck in a tree, and we would have never found them."

The longer the man swung the brush over Holly's face, the more her head filled with pleasant warmth. Revitalized, she propped herself up.

"Who are you?" she asked.

"This is Professor Gerald Kaplin, instructor of Healing Brushstrokes at Cliffony," LePawnee said.

"Are they all right?" Holly asked, glancing at the others who were spread out on a cobblestone path, moaning.

Kaplin nodded solemnly and slipped his brush back underneath his black cloak.

"And where is Ms. Hubbleworth?" Holly asked as she stood up.

"Professor Hubbleworth," corrected Mr. Kaplin, "she is back at Cliffony where she belongs."

Holly was about to ask Kaplin what he meant, when a short man with a grim look on his face and a bulging red scar across his forehead came running down the cobblestone path. Holly froze. It was the same man she had seen under the tree in Donkleywood with the cloaked creature.

"Mr. Kaplin, what is going on here?" said the man. His voice sounded nasally, and he was rolling his R's strongly.

Brian whirled around and glared at the man with hatred.

"This is Professor Farouche," said LePawnee. "He's the instructor of Unfinished Painting I."

Reluctantly, Holly shook Farouche's clammy hand. It felt like holding a dead eel in her hands.

"What happened here?" Farouche snarled.

"The children used MSP," Kaplin said calmly.

"I must report this to the High Council immediately. They are not allowed to own MSP." Farouche turned to Holly and Brian. "From where did you get it?"

"We found the jar lying in the dunes," Holly said, instinctively knowing it was better not to tell Farouche about the mysterious box.

"Mortimor, I think we shall discuss this later," interrupted LePawnee. "The children need to rest now."

The professor clapped her hands, and a carriage pulled by two griffins appeared from the twilight. The carriage was the shape of an egg, and Cliffony's coat of arms was carved into the wooden cabin doors. Two glass spheres at the front of the carriage lit the cobblestone street. Holly was amazed that the spheres were not illuminated by bulbs but instead by hundreds of fireflies that zoomed around inside.

A black-haired man stepped out of the carriage, holding a rusty lantern. He wore a tight gray shirt that showed off his muscles. A velvet cloak hung over his strong shoulders and dark eyes sparkled under his thick, black eyebrows.

"Oh, look at him," Amanda whispered. "Handsome."

She checked her makeup in the carriage window, fluffed up her bangs a bit, and went over to the man.

"Hi, I'm Amanda Heavenlock. And who are you?" She held out her hand, batting her eyelashes.

"What a flirt," Brian said.

The man reluctantly shook Amanda's hand. "I'm Christopher Bundo. I teach at Cliffony."

"Professor Bundo will take you to the hatchery," said

LePawnee. "We've decided that you will stay there until further notice."

"Everybody get in," said Bundo in his deep voice. "We want to get to the hatchery before it gets completely dark."

"What kind of hatchery?" Holly asked.

"The Griffin Hatchery," Bundo said.

Holly climbed into the carriage and made herself comfortable by the window, opposite Brian. Amanda elbowed her way in front to get the spot right next to Bundo, while Rufus sat by the door, reading the *Encyclopedia of Magora*.

"Get some rest. I will see you next week at Cliffony," LePawnee said as she waved at them.

The griffins pulled the carriage a few feet off the ground and accelerated forward. Tired, Holly sank into the soft velvet cushions. She wondered how she would get back to the real world. Not that she wanted to return to Donkleywood, but she couldn't live in a fantasy world forever, or she might become a fantasy figure herself.

At least she did not have to deal with the Smoralls anymore. By now, they were probably celebrating her disappearance anyhow.

Minutes later, Bundo was snoring, mouth wide open, head leaning back on the wooden panels.

"Don't you think it is strange that Farouche was in Donkleywood even though he's part of this painting?" Brian whispered to Holly.

Holly nodded. "Yes, it is. He said to the cloaked creature that he's after me. Maybe they came to Donkleywood because of me."

"Do you think he can go back and forth between the two worlds?" Brian asked.

"I have no idea," said Holly. "But I don't feel comfortable around him."

"Me either," Brian said.

Staring out of the window, Holly swallowed hard as she watched darkness engulf the lush meadows.

"I think Brian is right." Rufus looked up from the *Encyclopedia of Magora* and said, "It says here that the Duke of Cuspidor keeps fire-spitting seahorses as guards."

"That means Cuspidor is the one who is after me," Holly said. "It can't be a coincidence that the fire-spitting seahorses were in the same place where the fire broke out. Cuspidor probably sent them. He must have killed Grandpa Nikolas."

A surge of anger rose up in Holly, and tears welled up in her eyes.

"You must be a big threat to Cuspidor if he is trying so badly to get rid of you," said Rufus. "Maybe you really are a Gindar."

Holly wiped her tears. "But I'm not—I can't be a Gindar. It's a mistake. Don't you see? A Gindar is a highly gifted painter, and I don't have any talent."

Brian handed Holly a crumpled tissue. "You'll be all right. We're all on your side."

Just then, the carriage touched down with a jolt.

THE GALLERY OF WONDERS

Cookie the Troll

I learned to use colors in a way that they were not seen as colors anymore, but as part of a whole. Reality and fantasy were no longer divided by color.

Professor Bundo woke up, swung the door open, and climbed out. Holly pulled down the carriage window. Ahead of her was a farm comprised of one main building and dozens of wooden barns on stilts.

A woman sat on a bench beside the road. She was wearing a pink wig at least a foot high that looked like a tower of curls, and she had an overbite that exposed two front teeth.

"We're here," said Bundo. "Come meet Professor Lapia."

Holly hopped down from the carriage. As she landed on the cobblestones, a squawking bird swooped down on her. Holly ducked down, throwing her hands over her head.

"Jeepers, get away from me!" she cried.

"It is a macaw," Rufus said, plunging to the ground as the bird darted toward him.

The macaw turned, ascended, and plummeted once again.

"What a nasty thing," Brian said.

"But it has beautiful red feathers," Amanda said.

Just as she said that, the macaw shot at her horizontally, like a bullet.

"It better not ruin my hair," Amanda shrieked as she crawled underneath the carriage.

The target now out of immediate reach, the bird turned on Brian.

"Move over," demanded Brian, throwing himself on the ground and crawling on all fours next to Amanda under the carriage.

Holly jumped to the side, accidentally stepping in a griffin dropping, and took cover next to Brian and Amanda.

"Yuck," said Holly, wiping her boot against the wheel. "Look at this mess."

The macaw touched the ground, swung itself back up, and then disappeared.

"Lilly, what is this parrot doing here?" Professor Bundo asked the woman with the pink wig.

"It has been flying around here for quite a while," said the woman. "I have no idea where it came from."

Holly peered out from under the carriage and found herself eye-to-toe with the woman's feet. She was barefooted. Strange blisters that looked like suction cups grew out of her toes. The woman took a step forward and stepped right into the same

griffin dropping Holly had just squished.

"Yuck, that tastes horrible," she hollered.

"Tastes?" Brian asked.

"No, of course not," the woman corrected herself, laughing. "I mean, 'feels' horrible. You can come out now. The parrot is gone. Since it appeared today, it has been attacking almost everyone."

Holly crawled out from under the carriage, eyeing the woman skeptically. Never before had she met such a strange woman who seemed to taste with her feet.

"I think she's loony," Brian whispered to Holly.

"I'm Lilly Lapia, instructor of Creation and Deletion," the woman introduced herself and began to giggle like a child. "Nice clothes you are wearing," she said to Rufus.

"What is wrong with my clothes?" Rufus asked.

"Nothing," giggled Lapia. "You just look—so transparent."

"Transparent?" Rufus asked indignantly.

"Professor Lapia has some difficulties with her eyes," said Bundo. "She has a rare form of color blindness and can't see the color blue."

"And you must be wearing blue," said Lapia. "I don't see your body. You are nothing but a hovering head." She burst out in laughter.

Rufus didn't seem amused at all. He jerked his head back to Bundo. "Can we continue now?"

Bundo nodded.

"I will see you next week for the exam," Lapia hollered after them as they headed for the farmyard gate.

In the meantime, the sun had set behind the mountain range of Cuspidor. Multicolored stars illuminated the sky above. The smell of freshly mowed grass filled the air, and the crashing of the waves of Lake Santima echoed in the distance. Holly took a deep breath. She was free and happy. At that particular moment, she wanted to stay in Magora forever. But she knew that everything around her was a painting, and eventually she had to go back to reality.

Professor Bundo led them along a winding track past the barns on stilts. They reminded Holly of native Indonesian buildings she had seen in travel magazines. The path behind the barns was lined with birch trees leading to the gate which was flanked on either side by a limestone lion.

One of the lions snapped out of his frozen position. "What is your concern?" he asked.

Holly glanced at it warily. "Did it just speak?"

"Of course," said the professor. "All stone guards speak." He turned back to the stone lion. "I'm Christopher Bundo. I would like to speak to Cookie, the troll."

Rufus jumped back. "A t-t-troll?" he stuttered. "Trolls are dangerous. I have read in the *Encyclopedia of Magora* that trolls have attacked Magora many times. They are Cuspidor's allies."

Bundo laughed. "Not our Cookie. He's the most pleasant troll you have ever met. He was abandoned as a baby. LePawnee found him and brought him back to Magora. He was raised right here in the hatchery."

Grandpa Nikolas loved painting trolls. Holly remembered watching him many times when he sketched them out. He always said that he enjoyed making unpleasant things look

pleasant. It didn't surprise her that Grandpa Nikolas had come up with the idea of a friendly troll to add to his painting of Magora.

The stone lion leaned menacingly toward Bundo. "I will announce your arrival. But first, I want my reward," he roared, revealing his sharp limestone teeth. "One of these children would be fine."

Holly and Brian stumbled back a step; Amanda and Rufus hid behind Bundo.

"It is quite common for stone guards to ask for some kind of reward," whispered Bundo, "but I've never heard of one being so bloodthirsty. Usually they want pebbles."

"This time I want a child," growled the stone lion. "If you can't give me a whole child, give me an arm or maybe an ear to nibble on."

"Something is very wrong here," the professor whispered to Holly. Like a poisonous snake attacking its prey, Bundo darted forward, pulling out a needle from underneath his cloak. He stuck it into the lion's paw. The lion howled.

"Why does this hurt you?" asked Bundo. "Stone guards should not feel pain."

Growling, the lion whirled. A rumbling sound followed, and a dense cloud of fog engulfed the statue. As the fog vanished, so did the lion.

A massive troll cowered on the pedestal where the lion once stood. He was covered from top to bottom with short green hair. Only on his head the hair was orange and much longer. His brown eyes were tiny compared to the nose that was as thick as a flower bulb. He looked at them with a goofy smile.

"All right, you win this time," said the shape-shifter. He laughed. "I should have known that stone guards don't feel pain. But it was funny, wasn't it?"

"Not really," said Bundo, sourly. "Children, this is Cookie. He is a shape-shifter and can turn himself into whatever he likes, but he keeps the form of a troll most of the time. Unfortunately, he uses his talent in the most unprofessional way."

"Glad you guys made it," said Cookie. He pushed Bundo aside and gave Rufus and Amanda a big hug. He then grabbed Brian and cheerfully rubbed his knuckles on the boy's head.

"And this must be Gindar Holly O'Flanigan," said Cookie. He bowed toward Holly, gently took her hand, and kissed it. "So nice to meet you," he said.

"Just call me Holly," she said, embarrassed. "I'm not a Gindar. It's just a rumor."

"Oh, I like modesty," said Cookie, laying his arm around her shoulder. "And sorry if the lion prank scared you. It's just so much fun to be a shape-shifter. Come on, I'll show you your new home."

Professor Bundo turned around, waved goodbye, and walked back along the path. Cookie threw open the wrought iron gate, veered to the right onto a narrow path, and led them behind the farmhouse.

"Here's where you'll stay," announced Cookie.

Holly's mouth dropped wide open.

"Jeepers. Are we supposed to live in a tree?"

Villa Nonesuch

The line between reality and fantasy can be wavy or straight. It all depends on what path you want to take.

Agigantic birch tree grew in the middle of a large wheat field. The massive trunk was at least thirty feet wide. It had a wooden door with a face carved into it.

"This is Villa Nonesuch," said Cookie. "She's not a tree but a tree house. I hope you'll get along with her. She has her quirks, but usually she is very friendly." He walked through the wheat field to the birch, caressed the door gently, and planted a kiss on the giant nose.

Holly heard a friendly female voice as two tiny eyes opened up in the door. "You're such a charmer. You always know how to please an old lady."

Holly walked up to the tree house. "You can speak?" she

asked.

"Of course, my dear. I'm alive," said Villa Nonesuch, shaking her leaves. "And you must be Holly O'Flanigan—all of Magora is talking about the Gindar."

"I'm not really a Gindar," Holly said.

"Whatever, my dear. Come in and make yourself comfortable," Villa Nonesuch said.

The door swung open to a spacious living room. Almost everything inside was made out of birch. Even the sunflowers on the living room table and the clock above the fireplace were carved from the white wood.

"There are four bedrooms upstairs," said Cookie. "Villa Nonesuch will assign you each a room tonight." Cookie spun in a circle and began talking so fast that it was impossible to understand what he was saying. A cloud of fog encircled him and, with a boom, he turned into a giant banana.

"Fruits are on the upper shelf in the kitchen," said the banana. After more fog, there was another boom and a cow appeared. "Fresh milk is in the basement." With a third boom, Cookie became a lollipop. "I have some sweets for you in a jar on the kitchen table." Then with a boom, he was a donkey. Three more booms and he became a chicken, a stalk of broccoli, and then a carrot.

"Enough, enough," Holly finally said. "You're making me dizzy."

Cookie changed into his original troll form, said goodnight and, with another boom, buzzed out as a giant bumblebee.

"Boy, what a nutcase," Brian said, throwing himself into a recliner in front of the fireplace.

Holly was about to make herself comfortable on the soft, deep carpet when a screech upstairs made her jump.

"Stupid log cabin!" screamed Amanda. "Let me in there right now."

A door slammed, and Amanda came running down the stairs, her hands pressed against her forehead. "I hate this place."

The walls of Villa Nonesuch trembled. "I'm not a log cabin. I'm a tree house."

"What happened?" Brian asked.

"I wanted that big room overlooking the meadow, but the door slammed shut on me and it wouldn't open again," said Amanda. "So I kicked it."

"And I kicked back with the armoire door in the hallway," said Villa Nonesuch, banging a few kitchen cabinet doors open and shut.

"I think you will have to let Villa Nonesuch decide which room you will get," said Rufus. "The encyclopedia says that you should never go against the will of a tree house. They can make your life a living hell if they want."

"Sit down, Amanda," Holly said briskly. "We'll have to talk about some rules while we're in this painting."

"Do you think it's safe to talk in front of the tree house?" Amanda asked.

"What kind of tree house do you think I am?" said Villa Nonesuch, indignantly.

Rufus flipped the encyclopedia open and read, "'Tree houses have a pledge of secrecy regarding anything that is said and done within their trunks.'"

"All right then," said Holly. "I think we all know that we are in a painting. And this is a fantasy world. It's like dreaming—it's fine to do it at night, but you have to wake up in the morning."

Holly sighed. Losing touch with reality would eventually have consequences, as it would have if you never woke up from a dream.

"I think Holly is right," said Rufus. "If we stay, my parents will start worrying about where I am."

"I suggest we try to attract as little attention as we can while we are here," said Holly. "And in the meantime, we will try to find a way back. Do we all agree that we should get out of here as soon as possible?"

Brian and Rufus nodded.

Amanda crossed her arms and pursed her lips. "Since I've fallen into this stupid painting, I've bruised myself, gotten my hair ruined by a parrot, messed up my outfit by crawling underneath a carriage, and now I get a door slammed in my face by a silly tree house. I look like a wreck, and you wonder if I want to get out of here?" She tossed her hair over her shoulders and stomped upstairs. She squealed as two doors slammed. Then, there was silence.

"I think she agrees with you," Brian said.

"Let's go to bed," said Holly, yawning. "Tomorrow we can start to look around to see if we can find a way out of this painting."

She said goodnight to Brian and Rufus and trotted up the stairs. The door to the room that Amanda wanted so badly was open. Holly thanked Villa Nonesuch for the room and closed

the door behind her, wondering if Amanda was jealous that the tree house had given her the room.

It was cozy and warm inside. It felt as if she were walking on clouds when she stepped on the carpet in front of the intricately carved four-poster bed. The soft cushions and the flickering flames in the fireplace gave Holly a feeling of comfort and security. It almost felt as if she finally had a home. Tomorrow morning, she wouldn't encounter Ms. Smorall shouting and banging at the attic door. She wouldn't have to scrub and polish the floors, and she would not have to wake up on a dirty mattress.

Holly changed into the pajamas she found in the closet and climbed behind the scarlet velvet curtains of the four-poster bed. As she pulled the embroidered comforter up to her nose, the raspy voice she had heard twice before echoed through the room.

"Holly," it echoed.

Holly sat up, her skin covered with goose bumps. "What do you want?" she whispered, focusing on the open window. "I know who you are. Can you hear that voice?" Holly asked, hoping that Villa Nonesuch would respond. But obviously the tree house was already asleep.

The voice laughed wickedly. Holly jumped out of bed and darted to the window. All she saw was the reflection of the twinkling stars in Lake Santima. Everything else was peaceful. The ruin of the castle in the mountains of Cuspidor glowed under the light of the full moon.

"You must be Cuspidor," Holly called into the night sky. "What do you want from me?"

The voice laughed again and said, "The prophecy, Holly—the prophecy."

Holly slammed the window shut, jumped into the four-poster, and pulled the comforter up to her nose again. Sighing heavily, she closed her eyes.

Tomorrow, she would find out about this prophecy. But not now, she thought, and drifted into a deep sleep.

The Prophecy

I used to think that reality and fantasy were divided by a straight line, a very clear cut. But I learned that lines are more flexible.

Holly woke to a squawking noise coming from outside the tree house. She hopped out of the four-poster bed, swung the window wide open, and stuck her head out into the bright sunlight to find out what was going on.

Seven baby griffins, the size of full-grown pigs, hovered over the meadow below her. Cookie was standing between the griffins. Each one tried to stay in the air with tremendous effort, flapping its small wings. A black griffin with a white spot on his forehead puffed loudly and pushed himself up into the air, only to fall on his back with a thump. He tried once more and after a double back flip, he landed headfirst on the ground. Holly laughed out loud.

"Good morning. Did you have a good sleep?" Cookie called up as he ducked back and forth between the heavy griffins, trying not to get squashed by them.

"Good morning," said Holly. "What are you doing?"

"Dealing with problems, lots of problems," Cookie sighed. "They are already nine days old, and they still don't know how to fly. Usually griffins learn within three days, but these are a little slow."

Cookie petted the baby griffin with the white spot. "Whitespot is the worst. I have worked with him for days, but he doesn't seem to make any progress. Some never learn to fly. They end up being beasts of burden in the mines. Not a very pleasant prospect for a griffin."

As soon as Whitespot heard the word "mines," he flapped his wings in panic, swooped up into the sky, and stayed in the air for a few seconds. Then he fell headfirst to the ground and squawked heartbreakingly.

"Poor thing," Holly said.

"By the way, breakfast is in the kitchen," said Cookie.

Holly looked back and noticed that her clothes had been washed and neatly folded on a chair in the corner. She peeked into the closet opposite the bed. Holly's jaw dropped when she saw the shelves stacked from top to bottom with clothes.

"I hope everything is to your satisfaction, my dear," said Villa Nonesuch. "They are all your size." The shelves moved in and out, one at a time, as if giving her a quick inventory of her new wardrobe.

"Thank you so much," said Holly, stopping the nearest

shelf when the presentation began again.

"I was awarded the Medal of Honor for Housekeeping by the High Council," said Villa Nonesuch.

"What is the High Council?" Holly asked.

"It is a group of about twenty members," said Villa Nonesuch. "Everything in Magora is regulated by them. High Councilor Krah is the head of it."

"You will have to tell me more about the High Council sometime," said Holly as she left her bedroom.

She went downstairs. The smell of fresh croissants and chocolate filled the room. Piles of pancakes with blueberries and strawberries were stacked in the middle of the table. Scrambled, fried, and boiled eggs were set up around them. Chocolate pudding and pastries of all kinds were squeezed in between cheeses and sausages.

Holly sat down at the far end of the table and picked the most delicious looking croissant. At that precise moment, the croissant flipped around and whirled into the air. Holly jumped up and knocked her chair over backward. There was a boom, some fog, and the croissant changed shape.

"Cookie, stop that," cried Holly. "I was about to eat you."

"Wasn't that funny?" Cookie asked. "I've never been a croissant before."

"You scared the heck out of me," Holly said. "I could've broken my neck and—" she pursed her lips as if she had swallowed a bug, "I could've chewed a piece of troll ear."

"I'm sorry. I thought it would make you laugh. All I wanted was—" Cookie paused and orange tears began rolling down his troll cheeks. "I just wanted to make your day a little brighter," he said meekly.

"It's all right, Cookie. Forget it."

Smiling, Cookie dashed into the kitchen and removed the kettle from the stove. "The others had better come down soon, or the hot chocolate will get cold."

Five minutes later, Brian, Rufus, and Amanda were piling food onto their plates. Everybody looked well rested and relaxed. Holly thought it was the right time to ask about the prophecy.

Trying to sound casual, Holly said, "Cookie, have you heard about a prophecy in Magora? Oh, and could you pass the butter, please?"

Cookie dropped his fork that had been halfway to his mouth.

"What did you say?" he asked.

"I asked you if you could pass the butter," said Holly, innocently.

"No, how do you know there is a prophecy?" Cookie asked.

"There are always prophecies," Holly said.

She stirred her tea for the seventh time, trying to avoid looking at Cookie's face.

"Yes, there is one. Just a minute," Rufus said. He got up and went upstairs. There was an awkward silence until he returned with the *Encyclopedia of Magora* in his hands. "It is all in here. If you would spend more time reading, you would know. There's more in this book than I have ever learned in school."

Rufus opened the encyclopedia, flipped through the pages, and read out loud, "L, M, N, O, P—Propane, Property—here

it is, Prophecy. It says, 'There are many legends about the island of Magora. One widespread prophecy states that in the land of Cuspidor the Grand Gindar shall appear and will finish what was left unfinished. Interpretations of what the word "finish" could mean vary significantly. Some say that the Gindar will help Cuspidor finish his plan to destroy Magora. Others say that the Grand Gindar will destroy Cuspidor.'" Rufus shut the encyclopedia with a loud thud.

"And that Grand Gindar is Holly," Cookie said casually.

"Me?" Holly jumped up, knocking the chair over again. "Cookie, I've told you I'm not a Gindar."

"We'll see if you are a Gindar or not," he said. "Get your paintbrush."

Holly went back to her room and picked it up. She went back down and showed it to Cookie.

"Paint something," he said, smiling.

Irritated, Holly rolled the brush between her fingers. How could she create something without paint?

"Okay. I'll give it a try," said Holly. "Where is the paint?"

"Paint?" Cookie asked surprised. "You don't need that. You just have to put yourself in the mood, focus on the image, and apply the right brushstroke."

"Holly told you that she is not a Gindar," said Brian. "Why don't you get it? We don't really know how magic brushes work, so stop bugging us about this stuff."

Brian was a bit harsh sometimes, but he said what Holly was thinking. She was not a Gindar, and she was tired of hearing about it. Maybe being direct would stop Cookie from raising the issue again and again.

Cookie stood frozen. For the very first time he had a solemn look on his moss-green face. "B-b-but I thought you knew," stuttered Cookie. "I thought the Wise Man had told you."

"Told us what?" Brian asked. "We have never heard of the Wise Man. We know nothing."

Cookie dropped into the leather recliner. Big troll tears ran down his cheeks. "The Wise Man said there is a Gindar in Donkleywood who will save Magora. Without a Gindar, Cuspidor will destroy our land. Holly was our last hope. It's all over now. Magora will fall, and we will all die."

Creation and Deletion Brushstrokes

A line can meander. It can reach into reality and create peninsulas. In other places it can extend deep into the realm of fantasy.

Holly kneeled in front of Cookie, clasping his folded hands between hers. "Don't say that. We'll help you find the Grand Gindar."

"Yes, we will help you," said Rufus, placing his hands enthusiastically on Holly's.

"I guess we can do that," said Brian, placing his hand on Rufus'.

Amanda threw her hair back and sighed, "Oh well, I don't want to be a spoilsport. You can count on me, too." She placed her pinkie on top of the pile of hands.

Cookie raised his tear-stained face and smiled. "Thank you, my friends."

Throughout the following days, Holly and the others tried to find a way to help Cookie. But since they couldn't find an immediate solution for their problem of getting home, Holly walked around the hatchery and watched Whitespot continue to make efforts to fly. Rufus was completely absorbed in the *Encyclopedia of Magora*, while Brian climbed the branches of Villa Nonesuch. Most of the time, Amanda lay on the recliner with a cucumber mask on her face or fixed her nails.

One morning, Holly and Brian were grooming Whitespot outside Villa Nonesuch when Cookie called from the farmhouse, "Could you please come here for a moment?"

Holly and Brian went to the front porch where the shape-shifter was waiting in a rocking chair.

"I'm a bit worried," said Cookie. "Neither of you seem to know anything about magical painting. I don't even know if you have the skill to attend Cliffony. And next week is the entry exam. I don't want to know what chaos it'll cause when they find out Holly is not a Gindar—so you have to pass the test."

"You mean I will have to pretend to be a Gindar?" Holly asked.

Cookie nodded. "At least until we have found another solution to keep people calm."

"How exactly do you pretend to be a Gindar? And how are we supposed to pass the exam?" Brian asked.

"As long as she doesn't say she's not a Gindar everybody will assume she is," said Cookie. "And in the meantime I will try to teach you the basics of magic painting."

He called Rufus and Amanda and proposed the idea to them.

"Maybe I can get you through the exam," said Cookie. "I'm not a painter, but I have often seen how they do it. You have seven days of hard work ahead of you. Now follow me."

Cookie got up from the rocking chair and walked down the avenue of birch trees to the barns on stilts. Holly and her friends trailed behind. He climbed up the ladder of one of the smaller barns and flipped the hatch open. Then he crawled inside on all fours. Holly and her friends followed him. Cookie lit a few torches. In the dim light, Holly saw delicate carvings on wooden beams that supported a gabled roof. The barn was filled with hay bales.

"No one can find out what we are doing here," said Cookie. "That's why I nailed the windows shut. You can practice here without being disturbed or discovered."

Holly made herself comfortable on one of the hay bales. She was thrilled to have a class on painting. This was almost like going to Brushdale Art School, only that magic was involved. Now she could learn how to paint and become a true artist.

"Here are the three rules of magic brushes," said Cookie, holding up four brushes with a serious look on his face. "Rule number one—always keep your mind focused on the brush. Don't think about anything else but the brush and what you want to paint with it. Second rule—always create an exact image in your mind first. If you don't see it clearly, don't paint it. Third and last rule—use the correct brushstrokes. Even one incorrect brushstroke might get you a baboon instead of a griffin."

"What do you mean by creating the exact image in your mind?" Holly asked.

Cookie laid the brushes on the ground. "I'll show you. Look at this flowerpot," he said, picking up an empty clay pot from behind a pile of hay. "If you want to create such a pot, you will need to know every curve, blemish, and texture. And when you close your eyes, you should see all these details in front of you. The more realistic it looks in your mind, the more realistic it will come out."

Cookie swung the brush in the air.

"Then you circle the brush," he said. "Next, you use the correct brushstrokes. For a flowerpot it is a vertical line on the right, one on the left, and a horizontal line on the bottom."

After a boom and some fog, Cookie's body turned into a flowerpot with his head sitting in the soil like a pumpkin.

"Would you stop doing that?" Holly said. "There is not time for this."

"Just a little joke." Cookie changed back. "If I were an artist, the paint would have shot out of the brush and formed a flowerpot. Unfortunately, I'm not an artist, and so I can't show you." He kicked a few hay bales to the side, making space to practice. "Each object you create has a different brushstroke. You have to memorize them. But most important of all is your concentration. The better you can visualize the object you paint, the better the painting will turn out."

"Memorizing a stroke for every object?" Brian asked.

"What a bummer," added Holly, while Rufus' eyes sparkled in anticipation.

Brian picked up a brush from the desk. "Let's try this," he said, making a few strokes in the air.

Sparks shot out of Brian's brush, followed by gray paint

that hit Amanda right in the face. Amanda shrieked as the paint dripped off her nose and onto her freshly-ironed dress. "Oops, guess I didn't visualize it," said Brian, grinning.

"I'll get you for that," Amanda said through clenched teeth.

"Yes! You can do it, Brian," cried Cookie. "You didn't create a flowerpot, but you activated the brush. That means you can become a painter. Without talent, magic brushes don't react at all."

Amanda wiped the paint from her face, grabbed a brush, and swung it in the air.

Paint shot out of her brush, whirled around, and formed a flowerpot the size of a thimble. It hovered above them until it dropped on Brian's head.

"Oops, guess I missed the table." Amanda smiled devilishly.

"Yes, yes, yes," Cookie said delighted, "you can do it, too. It's a bit small for a flowerpot, but it's a good start, isn't it?"

Rufus picked up the third brush. "If she can do it, so can I." He waved his brush. Sparks shot out. Three lines of paint emerged in perfect alignment and created a gray flowerpot. The flowerpot settled gently on the desk. The perspective was a little off, but all in all it was a good effort.

"That's incredible," said Cookie. "You copy well. You could become a great Tracer."

Holly held on to one of the wooden posts that supported the roof. She felt sick, as if a stone in her stomach was weighing her down. How could she create something like that?

"Now it's your turn, Holly," Cookie said.

Holly mustered some courage and reluctantly picked up her brush. She made a brushstroke, but nothing happened. She tried it again. Nothing. Not a single spark.

"Here, try this one," said Brian, handing her his brush.

Holly made the three brushstrokes a third time. But again, nothing happened.

For many years she had thought she might have some hidden talent, but now it seemed that she did not have any. Maybe the Smoralls were right. Maybe they all were right and she should give up. Dismayed, Holly threw the brush into a hay bale. "I can't do it. I don't have any talent."

"Don't say that," said Cookie. "Maybe you are not concentrating enough. We'll practice."

"I don't think that is going to change anything. Everybody has always told me that I don't have talent," said Holly bitterly. "I guess they were right after all."

"Just because everybody told you that doesn't mean it's true," said Cookie. "Magical painting is something completely different. It requires patience and hard work. Some people might not develop their talent until later. I hope that is so with you."

Holly took a deep breath. Maybe she should give it a try. Never before had she been given the chance to take proper art classes. This was the chance of a lifetime.

The next seven days passed quickly. Every morning Holly studied brushstrokes and practiced them every afternoon. Brian quickly learned how to create a flowerpot, even though it always looked jagged. Rufus worked on his perspective skills, while Amanda struggled with size.

Holly, however, didn't improve. As much as she concentrated and practiced, she could never coax even a single spark out of the brush. She knew she would fail the entrance exam, just as she had almost failed this year's school in Donkleywood. But blowing the exam was not what bothered Holly the most—it was that she obviously had zero talent. For years she had believed the others were wrong—that she had talent but lacked the skills to show her creativity. Obviously, she had been wrong.

THE GALLERY OF WONDERS

Cliffony,
Academy of the Arts

Sometimes things might happen in your life that make you wonder if they are real. This is when the line curves and extends deep into reality.

A grunt woke Holly up. She opened her eyes and faced an orange snout. "Tenshi, get off me," she said, pushing the Nukimai gently off her chest.

Holly wiped cold sweat from her forehead. She had tossed and turned all night. What if everyone else passed the exam and she didn't? That would be mortifying. She crawled out of bed, went to the bathroom, and slipped into fresh clothes.

"Are you ready, Holly?" Cookie hollered from downstairs.

"Yes, I'm coming." She grabbed her backpack, kissed Tenshi goodbye, and darted downstairs.

As Holly sped past the kitchen, the cabinet door flung open and a brown bag full of sandwiches and muffins shot toward her. "You have to eat something," said Villa Nonesuch, as Holly caught the bag in midair.

Cookie was waiting on a maroon griffin. Brian, Rufus, and Amanda were sitting behind one another on a smaller one with a white spot on his forehead.

"Whitespot," said Holly, smiling. "So you finally learned how to fly."

She patted the creature's head. A few days before, Cookie had shown her how to ride a griffin. She got up on Whitespot's back and tightened the belt around her waist.

"Let's go, Maroon," commanded Cookie. The creature shot up into the sky like a rocket.

Holly held on to Whitespot's mane as he whizzed after Maroon. Whitespot made a delighted chortle as he dived like a roller coaster. He swung himself up again, only to dive back down a second later. For a moment, Holly forgot all her worries. She laughed and enjoyed the ride.

But as soon as the steep limestone turrets of Cliffony came into view, she remembered the exam. Whitespot circled twice above the courtyard and plummeted toward the giant entrance gate. Holly clung to his mane. Five feet above the ground, Whitespot made an abrupt ninety-degree turn. Like a plane on a runway, he gently landed, braking with his claws. A moment later, he came to a complete halt in front of the gate.

"Jeepers. What a ride," said Holly. "You sure have learned how to fly." Dizzy with excitement, she dismounted.

A skinny man with thick horn-rimmed glasses ran through

a crowd of kids who had been waiting on the stairs. His long purple cloak floated behind him.

"You can't park here," he yelled. "This is a no-stopping zone."

"I'll be gone in a minute," said Cookie. "Just dropping off the kids."

The skinny man pulled his thick glasses to the tip of his nose and scowled at Cookie. "Trolls," he mumbled with disdain, "shouldn't be allowed in the city."

Cookie mounted Maroon again. "Whitespot will be waiting for you in the parking zone at Market Square." Then he whispered, "That's Mr. Hickenbottom. He's the janitor at Cliffony. Don't mess with him. Last week he called the police on me just because I parked Maroon in the flamingo compound at the zoo."

"But griffins eat flamingos," Rufus pointed out.

"So that's why Maroon wasn't very hungry that night," Cookie replied.

"No more stopping here," shouted Mr. Hickenbottom. "If everyone stopped here, we'd have traffic chaos every day."

Cookie whistled, and Maroon shot into the sky, followed by Whitespot. In a matter of seconds, they disappeared in the distance.

"What are you waiting for?" snarled Mr. Hickenbottom. "Get in line. The gates will open in a few minutes. Fill out these forms and hand them to Professor Lapia." The janitor dropped a stack of questionnaires in Holly's hands and rushed back toward the massive gate.

"Professor Lapia?" Rufus said as he lined up behind a

few kids. "That is the strange woman who could not see my body."

"Yes," said Amanda, giggling, "and she didn't like the taste of the griffin poop."

Holly flipped through the questionnaire. These were weird questions, she thought. "'How many Q do you have at your disposal per term?'" she read aloud. "'When was the last time you donated blood?' 'Do you want to apply for a permit to visit the Gallery of Wonders?'"

"Just make something up," said Brian. "I always did that back in Donkleywood."

"You cannot do that," Rufus replied heatedly. "This might be vital information."

"Do you need some help?" asked a thin girl, sitting on the stairs. She was wearing a plain black dress that contrasted starkly with her pale white skin.

"Yes, that would be great," said Holly, relieved.

The girl jumped up, brushed her long, brown hair over her shoulder, and held out her hand. "My name is Ileana Kennicott."

Holly shook her hand, introduced herself, and handed Ileana the questionnaire.

"Have you applied before?" Ileana asked.

"No, it's our first time," Holly said.

"Mine too," said Ileana.

"Why haven't you applied before?" Holly asked.

Ileana's pale cheeks turned whiter than an eggshell. Nervously, she flipped through the questionnaires. "These are easy. 'How many Q do you have at your disposal per term?'"

Ileana read aloud.

"What on earth is a Q?" Brian asked.

"You are not from around here, are you?" Ileana asked.

"Nope, we got here a week ago," replied Brian.

Ileana pulled a little leather bag out of her pocket. She poured golden and silver cubes into her palm. "These are Q," she explained. "It's our currency. The smaller denominations are called Q-bits. Golden cubes are Q, silver cubes are Q-bits."

"We don't have any money," said Amanda, greedily staring at the gold and silver Qs in Ileana's hand.

"You get an allowance if you are accepted at Cliffony," said Ileana, "but some people have plenty of Q beforehand."

"Why do they ask us if we have donated blood?" Rufus asked.

Ileana nervously looked around. She pressed the silver medallion she was wearing tightly against her chest. "You see, there are 'other' people," she said, "I mean, creatures."

"What do you mean by 'other' people?" asked Holly.

She was a bit worried by the tone of Ileana's voice.

"In the past, Magora had some irresponsible Gindars," said Ileana. "They began painting people and animals, but never completed them. We call these creatures the Unfinished—half alive and half pencil drawing. They live life in a constant search for blood. Once they get enough blood, they can become a whole being. It takes a lot of blood though, and there are not enough donors in Magora, so—"

Ileana was interrupted by a loudspeaker. "New applicants, please have your papers ready. Exams will start shortly."

The stairs were immediately flooded with hundreds of

children running toward the gate while Holly and her friends filled out the rest of the questionnaire. Mr. Hickenbottom opened the right wing of the door. The crowd pushed forward. Holly stumbled up the stairs and into a gigantic entrance hall. A central staircase decorated with gargoyles and stone sculptures of griffins and dragons led up to a platform. There, the staircase split and continued on both sides. High above, a few rays of light shimmered through a circular stained-glass dome. They illuminated walls with stone carvings, which showed images of Magora.

When Holly reached the platform, the crowd split into two lines.

The familiar voice of Professor Bundo echoed through the speakers. "For medical examinations, boys to the left, girls to the right, please."

Holly squeezed herself between Amanda and Ileana, while Rufus and Brian lined up on the other staircase.

"Good to see you, Holly," said another familiar voice from the stairs above.

Holly's eyes wandered from a pair of bare feet to a towering pink wig.

"Professor Lapia," Amanda said.

"Could I please have your questionnaire?" said Lapia to Holly. "This exam will be a picnic for you."

Holly handed back the questionnaire without saying a word. She feared that if she said something, Professor Lapia would hear her voice trembling.

After a medical examination, an older student took Holly through a hallway with three ebony double doors. There, the

girls were reunited with the boys. A calm voice echoed through the speakers above. "The exam will start shortly. No shoving and no cutting in line. We expect orderly behavior."

"I need to go to the bathroom," said Ileana. She headed down one of the endless corridors that branched off from the hall.

"Wait for me," Holly and Amanda said at the same time.

Brian rolled his eyes, looking at Rufus. "I don't get it. Why do girls always go to the bathroom in groups?"

Holly and Amanda just looked at each other and laughed.

Rufus shrugged his shoulders, turning left into a hallway lined by suits of armor.

"We'd better hurry up or we'll miss the exam," said Ileana.

Halfway down the corridor, they came to an abrupt halt. A girl and a big, muscular boy blocked the way. The girl had intense black, slitted eyes. She reminded Holly of a snake. The boy was at least two years older, three heads taller, and his shoulders were as broad as Brian's and Rufus' together. He looked like a giant lizard with a protruding lower jaw.

"Well, if it isn't the Unfinished," said the girl with a strong hiss.

"Don't start that again, Gina," said Ileana.

"And who are these two? Losers like you?" said Gina, pointing at Holly and Amanda. "Don't you want to introduce us to them?"

"Holly and Amanda," said Ileana reluctantly, "this is Gina Chillingham and Lismahoon." Ileana pointed at the lizard boy. "His real name is Eric but everybody calls him by his last name."

"Holly O'Flanigan?" asked Gina. "Aren't we the new talent in town?" She leaned menacingly over, almost touching Holly's nose with her own. "I am the real talent in Magora, not you. So just remember that."

"That's enough," said Ileana. "Let us through."

With a devilish laugh, Gina pulled out a paintbrush from underneath her cloak. "Nobody tells Gina Chillingham what to do." She poked the brush into Ileana's face.

"Turn around now, and don't forget to take the one with the nasty hairdo with you."

Amanda put her hands on her hips. "Nasty hairdo?" she scoffed, insulted.

Gina hissed, and Lismahoon grabbed Holly and Ileana by the neck. Holly kicked with all her might against his legs, but to no avail.

Gina swung the brush and made a stroke.

Before Gina could finish the second circle, Amanda darted forward, holding her brush high in the air. She quickly drew three lines in the air.

A flowerpot appeared. With a thump, it fell on Gina's head and knocked her to the ground.

"Oops, I guess I'll never learn to land a flowerpot on the ground," said Amanda, grinning at Holly.

Lismahoon loosened his grip and darted to Gina.

"Thanks, Amanda," said Holly, rubbing her wrists. "Why did you do that?"

Amanda blushed and said indignantly, "Well, I don't have a nasty hairdo—besides, we have to stick together, don't we?"

Holly was speechless. Was Amanda her friend now? Before

she could say a word, the loudspeaker echoed above. "Last call for the entry exam."

"Come on, Holly," said Amanda, smiling, "let's go before Gina wakes up."

Holly smiled back. Maybe Amanda wasn't that bad after all.

The Exam

If unrealistic things happen, it is not because they happen without a reason. It is because you believed in them and allowed the line to enter the realm of reality.

Brian and Rufus were among the last students waiting to pass through the double doors.

"It's about time," said Brian as Holly breathlessly came to a halt in front of him. "I really wonder what it is about bathrooms that make girls want to spend half the day in them."

"Sorry, Gina stopped us," Holly said.

"Who?" Brian asked.

"Cuspidor is not the only nasty creature in Magora," said Holly. "I'll tell you about it later." She walked to one of the double doors. "By the way, Ileana, why did Gina call you an Unfinished?"

Ileana's eyes filled with tears. "Because I am one," she said.

Holly hesitated in front of the double door. "You don't look unfinished to me."

Ileana pressed the medallion tightly against her chest. "I was completed recently through blood donations," she said with a trembling voice. "Some people, like Gina, believe that after completion we formerly Unfinished aren't good enough to be part of Magora—they think that's the reason Gindars never completed us. But it's not true. Gindars are only human, and sometimes just forget to finish their tasks. Yet many people still treat us like outcasts."

Holly put her arm around Ileana and handed her a tissue she had in her pocket. "It doesn't matter to me," she said. "Where I come from my foster parents also treat me as an outcast. I don't care what you were. You're not an Unfinished anymore."

Ileana wiped her tears with the tissue. "Thanks, Holly," she said.

The loudspeaker blared again. "Exams will begin shortly. Please enter the Grand Hall."

Holly's pulse began to beat rapidly. For a split second, she had completely forgotten about the exam.

Brian placed his hand on Holly's shoulder. "Don't worry if you don't pass. We won't stay in Magora anyhow. As soon as we find a gate, we'll go back."

"I know," said Holly. She sighed as her head drooped. "But I have nothing to go back to. Grandpa Nikolas is gone, and I'm all alone. In Donkleywood I'm treated even worse than Ileana

is treated here. There is nothing to go back to in Donkleywood, and I have no talent to stay here in Cliffony."

"But you have something that many people do not have," Rufus said.

"And that is?" Holly asked.

"Dreams and imagination," said Rufus with a smile of admiration.

There was a minute of silence between them. Rufus put his arm around Holly's shoulder. "And you are not alone," he said. "I am here for you whenever you need me."

"And I'm here, too," Brian said.

"And I'm on your side whenever Gina bothers you," Amanda said.

Holly realized that she might not have the gift of creativity, but she had the gift of friends.

The double doors creaked and gradually closed.

"The opening ceremony is starting," Brian said as he put his foot in front of the door, holding it open for the others to pass. They all stepped inside.

Inside was a magnificent room with a vaulted ceiling. Gigantic brushes, their tips illuminated, hung from a ceiling that was as high as that of a cathedral. Stone columns supported the ceiling. They were cut in the shape of paint tubes, while the walls were covered from top to bottom with stone carvings depicting pencils, brushes, sketchpads—anything an artist could think of.

Hundreds of children were sitting on wooden benches. The benches were arranged in a half-circle around an elevated platform, which was shaped like a painter's palette. A few steps led up to the platform, behind which a beige silk curtain covered the wall; Cliffony's coat of arms was embroidered on it. Two long tables on either side of the platform seated about twenty people each—Cliffony's instructors. Professor LePawnee headed the right table with Lapia next to her. At the end of the table, Kaplin sat next to Bundo.

"Look who's there," said Holly, irritated. At the head of the left table was Professor Farouche.

"W-w-wait," Brian stuttered, obviously disturbed by something.

He pointed to the end of the table.

Holly stretched to look over the heads in front of her. Her mouth dropped wide open. Ms. Hubbleworth was sitting at the end of the left table. She was dressed in a garish pink outfit, and her top-heavy sunhat was decorated with brushes and paint tubes. The pink macaw that had attacked them the other day was swaying back and forth between the art supplies on her hat.

"Seems she likes her job now," Brian said.

"And I guess she found a friend in that nasty bird," Amanda added.

An usher hit a golden gong in the center of the platform. Professor LePawnee stood up. Silence fell over the hall.

"Every year, we gather to choose a few students to maintain and carry on the tradition of magic painting," the professor said. "Some of you will be chosen to attend Cliffony. If you are among the lucky ones, an intense four-year program will lie ahead of you. Some of you might become Tracers, others Legumers, and very rarely we have found Gindars among our

students." LePawnee paused and glanced through the rows of children, spotting Holly in the crowd.

Holly bit her lip, hoping that LePawnee would not mention her name.

But the Asian-looking woman smiled and continued, "This year we have the honor of having a Gindar among us." She pointed into Holly's direction.

The Grand Hall erupted in applause. Embarrassed, Holly slid down onto the bench, trying to hide from the crowd.

Professor LePawnee raised her hand. "I would like to welcome a few other students today who have not been able to attend Cliffony for centuries because of their impediment."

Relieved that her name was not mentioned, Holly sat up straight again.

"I'm glad to welcome a few former Unfinished," continued the professor. "Through your blood donations, we have been able to finish them."

A less jubilant cheer went through the crowd. Some boos accompanied the applause.

Professor LePawnee raised her hand again. "Silence. Before we start with the exam, I have an announcement to make. This school year, we will hold the Quadrennial Art Competition for the most talented students among you. We will inform you soon enough so that you can prepare yourself. There is also one more thing that might cause a bit of inconvenience. Due to renovations, the Gallery of Wonders has been closed until further notice. But now I'd like to introduce the instructors."

Holly poked Ileana on the bench in front of her. "What's the Gallery of Wonders?"

"It's a gateway," whispered Ileana. "The Gallery of Wonders is important for the survival of Magora. Every painting that was ever painted by a Gindar is stored in that gallery. Hundreds of worlds are depicted there; we call them gate paintings. If we need access to another world, we open one of these paintings and can enter without having to pass through the Land of Cuspidor."

"Why would you ever need to go to another world?" Brian asked.

"Because of Cuspidor," Ileana said. "We cannot create certain things. We have to rely on trade with other places. Cuspidor does not let anyone through his land. So we would be isolated if we didn't have those paintings."

"So that is why he wants to destroy the Gallery of Wonders," Holly said.

Her heart sunk. The island was surrounded by Cuspidor's empire, and there was no way out except for the gate paintings—and those were in the Gallery of Wonders which was closed.

"And now we will begin the selection process," Professor LePawnee announced. "Gullveig, the wise oracle, will help us with this difficult task." She pulled on a rope, and the curtain moved up, revealing a cave entrance five times as tall as Holly.

Professor Farouche strode onto the center of the platform. "When I announce your name, step into the oracle and do as you are told. You will be called in alphabetical order."

The gong echoed through the Grand Hall.

Oracle Gullveig

The line can be blurry or sharp. It all depends on how you make it.

Farouche called Serafina Abby. A red-haired girl with pigtails stepped nervously out from the last row and trotted up to the cave entrance. Farouche handed her a brush. Serafina hesitantly entered and was instantly out of sight. Two minutes of silence went by. Then Serafina stepped out onto the platform and drew a half-circle in the air. Paint shot from her brush and a mouse gray banana appeared on the platform.

"Tracer," echoed Gullveig's voice in the hall. Applause followed.

Professor LePawnee congratulated Serafina and sent her to the first row of benches that were reserved for the students who had passed.

Holly wondered if there was someone in the cave who had told Serafina what to do. Maybe this person would also tell Holly what to do. She knew she would find out soon.

A few other students went through the same process until they reached the letter "C."

"Gina Chillingham," Professor Farouche called.

Holly and Amanda scowled as Gina climbed up the stairs.

"I hope she fails," Amanda said.

"I doubt it," said Ileana. "Gina is the most promising talent in Magora. At least, she was until Holly showed up."

Holly didn't feel like competing, but Gina seemed to be ready for it.

She glanced at Holly and grinned arrogantly before she went into the cave. Less than a minute later, she strutted out and activated her brush.

A vegetable that looked like a cross between a light-gray carrot and a mouse-gray potato landed on the platform. Gina swung the brush. The potato-carrot disappeared and a bench formed. It looked exactly like the one Holly was sitting on, only that it was gray again. Gina sat down on the bench.

Gullveig's voice echoed from deep inside the cave, "Legumer." The Grand Hall erupted into applause. "And Tracer," added Gullveig.

"Didn't I tell you?" Ileana said. "Gina couldn't fail. She is destined to become something great. It is rare to find both talents in one person. She might even have Gindar qualities. We will find out about that once she has grown up."

Holly wondered if the same applied to her. If Gina could become a Gindar, then maybe she would have to get older first

for her talent to show.

"Why is Gina both a Legumer and a Tracer?" Brian asked.

"She was able to paint a new kind of vegetable," said Ileana, "something nobody had ever thought of before. It shows her creativity. And also by creating a bench, she showed that she can copy objects like a Tracer."

"But it's not an exact copy of the bench," said Brian. "It doesn't have color."

"Right," said Ileana. "Beginners can't paint in color here in Magora. Only advanced students know how to do that."

"Okay," said Brian. "I've never thought of that. Everything I've created has been gray so far."

"Students only learn to apply color to shapes in the second year," explained Ileana. "First you have to learn how to get the shapes right."

The gong echoed continuously. A short, fragile boy came out and swung his brush. A few drops of paint came out of the tip of his brush. They dripped down and made a big gray blob on the ground. Some students laughed. The boy's head drooped and, with tears in his eyes, he ran back to his bench. But he was not an exception. Many students failed the exam.

"Tell me again why we are putting ourselves through this?" Brian asked. "We are supposed to be in a magical world. Fantasy worlds don't have exams."

"Who says that?" Rufus asked. "If you dislike it, create your own fantasy world."

"And why are we taking an exam in a world that isn't even real?" Amanda asked.

"Because we like tests," Rufus said.

"Maybe *you* do," Brian replied, "but I don't."

"Stop it," said Holly. "No matter if you like tests or not, we owe it to Cookie to try."

Rufus and Brian stopped arguing.

"Christopher Fontanaire," Farouche called the next student.

Holly broke out in sweat. Only nine more letters and she would have to take the test. Her heart was pounding as she wiped the sweat from her forehead. She would soon become the laughing stock of Magora.

After Christopher had miserably failed his exam and ran out of the Grand Hall, Holly turned to Brian. "I think you're next."

At that precise moment, Farouche called Brian's name. Holly watched the professor as he wiped across his fleshy scar and grinned.

"Be careful," Holly said.

Amidst a volley of good wishes from his friends, Brian walked up the stairs, grabbed the brush from LePawnee, and darted into the cave. Two minutes later, Brian stepped back out onto the platform and drew a few curvy lines and some dots in the air.

Rufus was astonished, and he flipped through his notebook. "Curvy lines and dots? Those are not valid brushstrokes."

A cloud of paint formed on the platform. It whirled around and created an oddly-shaped table with a wide leg in the center that set itself down with a thump. The tabletop looked as if a dozen dogs had slobbered all over the dishes and glasses.

Amanda giggled. "What a mess. That's embarrassing. And

the perspective on the table is off, too."

The instructors didn't appear to object to the creation. On the contrary, they eyed the object with a great deal of interest.

"What is it?" LePawnee asked.

Brian pushed a button under the tabletop, and two metallic arms shot out from the central leg. The arms collected the dirty dishes, opened a latch in the leg, and placed the dishes and glasses inside.

"It's a table with a dishwasher inside," said Brian, rocking nervously from one foot to the other.

"Legumer," echoed out of the cave.

Holly jumped up from her bench and applauded. She was so relieved that her best friend had made it through the exam, but at the same time she felt a bit envious that he'd had such an easy time creating something.

Brian walked to the first row. The gong sounded again.

"Amanda Heavenlock."

Amanda didn't take more than a few seconds in the cave. Then, she stepped confidently out onto the platform and drew a half-circle and a few curved lines in the air.

"What kind of brushstrokes are those?" Rufus asked, once again, confused. "Where did she get all these ideas from?"

A golden helmet with four tentacles formed in the air. The lines were clean, and the shape was well done. Amanda snatched the hovering helmet out of the air, placed it on her head, and flipped a lever. The tentacles swung around the helmet like an octopus, pulling out cotton balls, makeup, and eyeliner from little compartments in the helmet.

Brian rolled his eyes, looking back over his shoulder at

Holly.

"Can you believe that? She created a portable beauty salon," Rufus said.

"Legumer," announced Gullveig.

Holly was excited that Amanda had passed, but this raised the bar even higher now. She would have to pass this exam so that she wouldn't look like a total idiot compared to her friends.

Ileana's name was called. After coming out of the cave, she lifted her brush and created a tree with paper boxes growing at the end of the branches.

"They look like to-go boxes from a Chinese restaurant," Holly said.

"I think you are right," said Rufus. "She created a Chinese fast food tree."

Ileana was announced as a Legumer.

Holly applauded again, but now she was more scared than before. With every student who made it through the exam, Holly's heart sank deeper. The more people passed the more of an embarrassment it would be if she failed.

Rufus' name was called. Holly grabbed his hand. "Good luck," she said.

Rufus climbed the stairs to the platform.

Holly was left alone on the bench. She counted L – M – N – O. Only four more letters. Her heart turned over.

After Rufus had come out of the cave, he calmly drew three circles in the air.

As Holly had expected, Rufus used the flowerpot brushstroke. He wouldn't have come up with something

original. A perfectly shaped mouse-gray flowerpot without any perspective mistakes floated down.

"Tracer," Gullveig hollered immediately.

A few other children were called. Then, the gong clanged louder than ever.

"Holly O'Flanigan," called Farouche.

Under earsplitting applause, Holly trudged to the platform. Farouche pushed her toward the cave. Holly stepped inside. The ground was slippery. She ran her hand along the wall so she wouldn't fall.

"Come in a little farther," Gullveig's voice reverberated in the tunnel.

It was pitch black as Holly moved deeper into the cave.

"Now I can see you better," Gullveig said calmly.

It took a few minutes for Holly's eyes to adjust in the darkness. There was an outline of a face in the distance.

"So you are Holly O'Flanigan—the one everybody has been talking about."

"Yes, but there must be a mistake," said Holly. "See, I'm not what everybody thinks I am."

The outline of the face in the distance came closer. It looked like a giant serpent, but as Gullveig approached, Holly realized it was not a snake.

"Jeepers. You're a tortoise," said Holly, surprised.

The long, wrinkled neck swung above Holly until two big eyes approached her and stopped right in front of her.

"Yes, I am a tortoise," said Gullveig. "And you are inside my shell."

Holly looked at the walls around her and understood

that this was not a cave. She had walked into the front of the tortoise's shell.

"You have to go out there now and show everyone that you are a Gindar," said Gullveig.

"But I'm not," Holly replied, meekly. "I've been trying to create a flowerpot, but it has never worked."

"Did you concentrate on the flowerpot itself?" Gullveig asked.

Holly nodded.

"No, I mean, did you really concentrate on the flowerpot? Or did you concentrate on what you wanted the flowerpot to be?" Gullveig's head hovered above Holly, swinging in smooth rhythm back and forth.

"Well, not really," muttered Holly. "I kept thinking that it would be much more interesting if the flowerpot looked prettier, or if it even became something completely new."

"And there is your mistake," said Gullveig. "Your concentration was sidetracked by what you *should* create, which was different from what you *wanted* to create. So the brush did not react. When you go out there now, try something different. Concentrate only on what you *want* to create, but this time nobody is telling you that you have to paint a flowerpot. Go with whatever you feel like and invent a brushstroke." Gullveig's head slowly vanished in the dark. "It's in your hands now. Good luck, Holly."

The Tower of Bats

A blurry line allows a smooth transition between fantasy and reality.

Hundreds of eyes stared at Holly when she emerged from Gullveig's shell. She tried lifting the brush, but her arm fell right back down; she was trembling. Gullveig's voice kept echoing in her mind, "Concentrate only on what you *want* to create."

What did she really want to paint? Holly remembered how she had tried a dozen times to paint the flowerpot. It would be useless to try that again.

She focused, and suddenly she knew what she wanted to create. Instinctively, her arm swung up, and she drew a few lines in the air.

White paint shot out like a jet stream. Holly gasped at the

brush. Had she actually activated it? The paint whirled around like a tornado and formed a fountain that spurted paint up to the ceiling. As the crowd murmured, Holly stumbled backward away from the white fountain, which grew bigger by the second. Sparks illuminated the Grand Hall so brightly that the professors shaded their eyes.

Had she really created this fountain? Had this stunning spectacle of lights actually come from her mind? Holly was dumbfounded.

The miracle lasted a few more seconds. Then it ended. The sparks poured down into a thread of mouse-gray mud. The fountain collapsed, spattering paint all over the professors. Students in the first rows crawled under their benches, while others took cover behind the stone pillars in the last rows. Holly sat on the ground with an ungracious thud and covered her face. She had failed again. There was complete silence.

Holly didn't want to look up, knowing that hundreds of disappointed faces would be staring at her. Maybe they would even be angry.

Amanda giggled in the first row.

Then she heard Brian breaking the silence, "What did she do?"

Holly peeked through her fingers while still sitting on the floor. The kids moved toward the platform. Some were standing on the benches, while others leaned over the shoulders of their fellow students. The professors had risen from their chairs.

"Why on earth is everybody so curious about that thing?" Amanda voice sounded. "It looks disgusting."

A squelch redirected Holly's attention to what was left of

her magnificent fountain. A paint-covered creature the size of a cat emerged from the puddle. It was a clay flowerpot with a Nukimai head. Reproachfully, the creature stared at its creator.

Holly uncovered her face, realizing that she had actually created something. She felt like jumping up and cheering, but the silence of the crowd stopped her. She glanced at the instructors, who stood frozen, seemingly unaware of the paint in their faces.

Holly lifted the brush, assuming she should get rid of the flowerpot-Nukimai. The paint that was spattered all over the place was sucked back into the tip. The flowerpot-Nukimai dissolved and vanished.

The Grand Hall filled with the loudest applause Holly had ever heard. She stared at the howling crowd in astonishment. What had gotten into them? Even the professors applauded.

Growling, Gullveig silenced the crowd.

Holly squeezed her eyes shut and crossed her fingers behind her back. "Please, please let me pass."

"Gindar," Gullveig's voice echoed through the Grand Hall.

Another wave of applause erupted. Brian, Rufus, and a few other boys jumped up from the first row, darted to Holly, and lifted her up into the air.

"Congratulations!" Ileana shouted up to her. "Nobody has created a living being, other than a plant, in a long time."

Holly shook her head. She had tried so many times and never had anything like that happened before. It must have been an accident.

"I'm not a Gindar," she mumbled.

But nobody listened to her. Each professor congratulated Holly, and the crowd shouted, "Long live our new Gindar!"

Finally, the boys set her down, and Holly stepped down from the platform. Holly was relieved, no matter if she was really a Gindar or not. For the first time in her life she had received applause for what she had created. At this very moment she stopped worrying and enjoyed her success.

Half an hour later, the last applicants had taken their exam. Professor LePawnee dismissed the students, telling them to pick up their schedules in the Tower of Bats and said goodbye to the students who had failed.

Holly and her friends left the Grand Hall. Ileana led them swiftly through a maze of hallways until they reached a steep spiral staircase. She told them it led up to the Tower of Bats.

Rufus stopped. "Wait. Holly, tell us how you created that flowerpot-Nukimai."

"Gullveig told me that I have to concentrate on what I *want* to create," said Holly. "I was always concentrating on what I *should* create. I made up the brushstroke and concentrated on my own idea. And it worked."

"That is amazing," Rufus said.

"That probably only worked because you created something completely new," said Ileana. "Usually every single thing has a specific brushstroke. If you don't use the right one, you either get nothing or, for example, toilet paper instead of a silk scarf. But we'd better pick up the schedules before the crowd rolls in."

They climbed the spiral staircase to the fifth floor, stopping

at a rusty metal door. Screeches echoed from behind it. Ileana swung it open. Holly ducked as dozens of bats shot out from the darkness.

Amanda threw her arms over her head, shrieking. "They are going to ruin my hair."

"Don't worry, they don't do anything," said Ileana. "My brother told me that Professor Gobeli loves bats, and they do whatever she says."

Surrounded by fluttering bats, Holly and her friends stepped into a round chamber filled with shelves. They were stacked high with antique books and papers. At a massive desk, a stout woman was flipping through a towering stack of parchment. A candle flickered next to her, flooding the chamber with a dim light. The woman was bald except for two long braids that started above her ears and reached all the way to her knees.

"This is Professor Gobeli," whispered Ileana, stepping into the light for the teacher to see her.

The woman pulled down her reading glasses and dropped the stack of parchment on her desk. "You are quite early. First-year students usually take longer finding their way up here." She tossed her braids over her shoulders and went over to one of the shelves. "Let me get your schedules." She pulled out a leather box. "Ileana Kennicott," she mumbled as she flipped through the papers in the box. "And who else is here?" Gobeli croaked, looking past Ileana right at Holly.

Holly stepped into the candlelight. "I'm Holly O'Flanigan."

A strange smile flitted over the professor's lips. Holly felt uncomfortable. She couldn't tell whether her new teacher was being friendly or not. Gobeli climbed one of the ladders leaning against the shelves and threw down a few velvet pouches, which landed with a loud clank on her desk. She stepped down from the ladder.

"Here is your schedule. And your monthly allowance," said the professor as she handed Holly a paper and a pouch.

Holly dropped the pouch into her pocket. "Let's go. I don't like it here," she whispered into Ileana's ear.

"And Holly," said Gobeli with an ominous tone in her voice. "Be careful. Don't think you are invincible now. Gindars can die like anyone else."

Holly nodded and ran down the staircase.

"Watch out. Gindars can die like anyone else," said Brian, mimicking Gobeli as they headed for the Student ID Department. "Was she threatening you? What was that old crow trying to say?"

"There is definitely something eerie about her," Rufus said.

"Yes," said Holly. "But I can't put my finger on what it is besides the fact that she looks weird."

In the Student ID Department, five boys were sitting in front of easels. Students had formed a line at each of the easels.

"Who are they?" Holly asked.

"Just a few Tracers," said a boy in a uniform at the entrance door. "Line up to get your ID."

"Thanks," said Holly. She picked the line closest to her.

When she got to one of the Tracers, he swung his brush and painted a miniature 3D image of her.

"You can pick it up at the end of the line," said the boy in the uniform. "Next."

Holly continued until she reached an athletic-looking student. "No pushing—everyone will get their ID," said the boy with a smug look on his face. He looked at Serafina Abby, the girl who had passed the exam first. "And take that lollipop out of your mouth."

Serafina froze on the spot. Her jaw dropped and the lollipop fell out of her mouth and onto the floor.

"Oh, leave her alone, Calvin," Ileana said.

"Sister dear, everybody should learn to respect third-year students," Calvin said.

"Yeah, right. Provided they are not your egghead brother," said Ileana, punching him playfully on the chest.

Holly picked up her completed photo ID, which was the coolest and strangest ID she'd ever seen. It was a tiny glass cube with a three-dimensional image of her head inside. She strolled down the hallway. "Calvin is your brother?" she asked Ileana.

"Yes, he can be a real pain in the butt. Ever since he became Cliffony's Best Artist, he thinks he can order everybody around. But having a brother like him also has its advantages."

"And they are?" Holly asked.

"He has shown me every corner of Cliffony," said Ileana. "That's why I know this place so well."

"I guess we're done till Monday," Brian said, looking down at his schedule. He was noticeably relieved.

"Let's go back to Villa Nonesuch," Amanda said.

"I'll take you back to the griffin parking lot at the market square," Ileana said. She led them through a maze of hallways lit by torches. "Each hallway has a name that relates to the subject of painting," she explained. "There is a sign at each corner." She pointed at an enameled sign that read, "Bristle Brush Hallway."

"Just remember the names, and you'll find your way around."

As they passed Canvas Corridor, Cuspidor's raspy voice echoed in the distance again. "Holly."

Holly stopped abruptly and glanced at her friends. It did not seem that they had heard the voice. Her heart began beating faster. Was Cuspidor inside Cliffony? Or was she just hearing the voice in her head again?

"Is everything all right?" Rufus asked.

"No, let's go down this way," Holly said, realizing the voice was coming from that direction. She sped down Canvas Corridor, veered to the left, and found herself facing huge double doors guarded by a giant stone sphinx.

Ileana came running after her, followed by Holly's friends.

"Don't go near the sphinx," shouted Ileana down the hallway. "It can kill you."

"What is wrong, Holly?" Rufus asked.

Holly ignored Rufus' question. "What is this place?" she asked, pointing at the door.

"This is the entrance to the Gallery of Wonders," Ileana said.

Ravenscraig Lane

We fear a smooth transition between fantasy and reality because the people around us don't see fantasy as a part of reality and so they might laugh at us.

Holly turned back to the double doors and stared at the sphinx. It was at least ten feet tall and made out of a red stone. Its face was that of a young man with a beard.

Suddenly, the eyes opened and it furrowed his forehead.

"What are you staring at? Haven't you seen a sphinx before?" it asked as it leaned forward to stare back at her. Holly could see her scared reflection in the flickering red eyes of the creature.

"Would you please let me enter the gallery?" Holly asked.

"I have strict instructions not to let anyone through," he said, turning away from her.

"But there's someone inside who is not supposed to be in there," Holly replied, assuming that Cuspidor must be close.

"That can't be. I haven't left the door for a moment," the sphinx said.

"I believe there is someone in there," Holly insisted. "I heard a voice."

"A sphinx always asks questions that you have to answer," said Rufus. "You might want to try that to get in."

"Stupid old clichés," the sphinx said, growling and raising one of his sharp claws. "I can decide myself whether I let someone through or not. And I don't see a reason why I should let you in."

Brian pulled Holly back. "Didn't you hear what he said? I think you should forget about it. Besides, I didn't hear any voice."

Another growl was all it took to convince Holly that it wasn't a good idea to argue with something that was five feet taller, had razor-sharp teeth, and claws like knives. She backed off. She would not be able to pass the sphinx today, but she would try to think of a plan to outwit the creature.

Holly followed Ileana out of the maze of hallways. Ten minutes later, they had left Cliffony and were standing on the stairs where Cookie had dropped them off earlier. Holly noticed a blue enameled sign that pointed down the hill. It read Papplewick Street.

It had the same name as the street in Donkleywood, only that it ended in the word "street" and not in "road." Holly realized that Grandpa Nikolas must have taken the name from the real world.

However, while strolling down Papplewick Street, Holly noticed it was very different from Papplewick Road. Like a snail shell, it wound around the hill, passing small shops that sold everything from magic brushes to baby griffins. The people who were shopping on the street looked as strange as the objects sold in the stores. Ledesmas and dwarfs mingled with humans wearing cloaks and pointed hats. Their outfits looked more like Halloween costumes than everyday clothing.

Passing Holly, Rufus rushed off as soon as he spotted the magic bookstore. Then, Brian ran to the baby griffin store, and Amanda disappeared into Wrinkle Dimple Skincare Shop.

The smell of fresh pastries from a nearby bakery caught Holly's attention. She was drawn to the front window, which had an amazing display of the island of Magora, completely made out of candy. Chocolate butterflies and tiny griffins made out of marzipan fluttered back and forth above Cliffony. Caramel-coated rabbits nibbled on plants made of blue meringue. Holly's nose was glued to the window pane.

Ileana tapped Holly on the back. "Do you like pastries?"

"They look yummy," Holly said.

"So why don't we get some?" suggested Ileana. "We have our monthly allowance." She jingled the pouch that Professor Gobeli had given her and poured three golden cubes of different sizes into her palm.

Holly opened her pouch and they both looked inside. Twenty-five cubes of all sizes were inside.

"That can't be," said Ileana, pouring her own cubes back into her pouch. "They must have made a mistake."

"What do you mean?" Holly asked.

Ileana counted Holly's cubes. "You've got 2400 Q. See, one of these large cubes is worth 500 Q," she explained. "The medium one is 100. The smaller is worth one Q. The silver cubes are Q-bits." Ileana jingled her pouch. "Look, I only have 300 Q. That's the average allowance."

"Jeepers. I'm rich," hollered Holly, jumping into the air. The shout scared the marzipan griffins in the window, causing them to hide in one of the meringue trees.

Holly paused, her head drooping. "I'd better take it back. It's not right to keep it. Professor Gobeli must have made a mistake."

"Wait a minute," said Ileana as she looked into Holly's pouch. "There's a paper inside."

Ileana reached into the pouch and pulled out a piece of parchment. She unfolded it and read aloud,

Dear Holly,
Nikolas O'Flanigan accumulated a large fortune. He wanted you to have it. You will get a monthly allowance of 2500 Q until you are of age. Then, the whole fortune will be handed over to you.
Best regards,
Professor LePawnee.

"I guess you really are rich," Ileana said.

"Jeepers," Holly cried, once again startling the marzipan griffins, which shot from the meringue tree into a pudding mountain. "Imagine what I can do with all this money."

Holly hopped around in a circle, holding the pouch high over her head. "I'm rich, I'm rich!" she cheered. "Let's go and

get some pastries."

Holly flung open the door of the bakery and stepped inside. A tiny bell chimed a little tune from atop the door.

The smell of chocolate and croissants greeted Holly and Ileana as they entered the bakery.

"Let's get some marzipan griffins," said Ileana, staring at a nut-covered miniature griffin hovering over her head.

The shop was stuffed from top to bottom with cakes, pastries, and anything someone with a sweet-tooth could desire. In the farthest corner was a counter made of gingerbread. Holly squeezed between a nougat castle and a steam locomotive made out of chocolate.

"Anybody here?" she called, as she reached the gingerbread counter.

A slurping noise came from behind the counter and a wrinkled face appeared.

"Howdy," said the face.

It belonged to a dwarf with a bushy white beard and a pointed hat. He was holding a chocolate snail that was overflowing with green liquid.

"What is that?" Holly asked.

"It's my new recipe," said the dwarf. "Green mango syrup. It's delicious—wanna try?"

"No thanks, but we would like some of those marzipan griffins," Holly said.

"Very good choice. I invented that many years ago. It is still the top seller."

"How much are they?" Ileana asked.

"1.99 Q," replied the dwarf.

"I'll take five," said Holly.

The dwarf disappeared into the backroom and returned with a butterfly net. He skipped around the store, trying to catch the flying griffins. Holly laughed. She hadn't expected him to catch the ones flying around but had thought they would be stored in jars somewhere.

Holly poured her Q into her palm. "I'll treat you," she said to Ileana. She picked a large golden Q. "Is this enough?"

"Are you crazy? That's 100 Q. Use that one." Ileana pointed to a smaller cube.

The dwarf wobbled back with five marzipan griffins in his net. They were no longer moving but looked like ordinary candy. The dwarf wrapped them up in brown paper. Holly dropped the other cubes back into her pouch.

The 10 Q cube in her hand suddenly bounced up and down. It spun around twice, and a latch opened on its top. A man the size of a tiny beetle peeked out. He was dressed like a judge with a black robe and a white wig. The little man cleared his throat and pulled down his reading glasses.

"You sure have sufficient funds, but don't spend it lavishly on unhealthy food or unnecessary items," said the man. "School supplies will cost you more than you expect. Still, I give you my permission."

The man bowed, disappeared into the box, and snapped the lid shut.

"What on earth was that?" Holly asked.

"It's just the Q people," said Ileana. "They keep track of your finances. If you don't have enough money, they suggest you save it. They can be quite annoying sometimes. You don't

have to follow their advice though. Most people don't."

Skeptically, Holly examined the cube, tapped it a few times, and handed it to the dwarf.

"It's getting dark," said Ileana. "We'd better get going."

Holly grabbed her purchase and hurried out of the bakery. A few minutes later, she found Brian, Rufus, and Amanda strolling down Papplewick Street.

"I found the best fake eyelashes you have ever seen," Amanda boasted, batting a pair of long crimson eyelashes.

Holly stopped in the middle of the street. There was a murmur somewhere far in the distance. Holly looked past Amanda into a dark alley. The murmur got louder and turned into a voice but it was still so far away that Holly didn't understand what it was saying. She had the uncomfortable feeling that it was Cuspidor.

"What is it?" asked Amanda, looking right at Holly.

A shiver went down Holly's spine. "I think Cuspidor is in that alley," she said.

"How do you know that?" Amanda asked as she took a step back.

"I have been hearing his voice for quite a while," explained Holly. "He's been talking to me."

Amanda, Brian, and Rufus stared at her silently.

"I'm not crazy," said Holly. "And don't ask me why I can hear him. I just can."

Holly turned away from her friends and looked down the alley again.

It was a narrow street with dilapidated buildings. Shops were boarded up with wooden planks. About thirty feet into the alley, the street took a ninety-degree turn, blocking their view.

"That's Ravenscraig Lane," said Ileana with a tremble in her voice. "You don't want to go in there. That is where evil things are sold. It can be dangerous."

"I have to find out what Cuspidor wants from me," said Holly. "He might be right around that corner."

Holly ignored Ileana's advice. As she headed toward Ravenscraig Lane, her heart started pounding and fear filled her whole body. What would she find around the corner in the tiny alley?

Professor Lapia's Class

People might consider us crazy because we live in a world undivided by the line.

The closer Holly drew to Ravenscraig Lane, the shakier her legs felt. She was scared of what she might find. She held on to a lamppost and took a deep breath.

"Stop," shouted a voice from above.

All of a sudden, the lamppost moved a few inches. Holly shrank back and looked up. A giant, dressed in shiny armor, glanced warily down at her.

"I'm sorry," said Holly as soon as she realized that the lamppost was the giant's leg.

"Password please," growled the giant.

Ileana pulled Holly back by her sweater. "Ravenscraig Lane is dangerous. You need a password to get in. Let's go home."

"All right. I don't think the giant would let us through anyhow," said Holly, relieved that she had an excuse not to go into the alley.

They continued wandering down Papplewick Street. Approaching Market Square, they saw Whitespot in the parking area surrounded by other griffins. Holly and her friends hopped on his back and said goodbye to Ileana. As soon as they had done so, they found themselves flying up into the evening sky. A breeze of the air caressed Holly's face when they shot through the clouds. For a moment, she felt free from all her problems. She no longer had to worry about passing the exam or being locked in the attic by the Smoralls. If it hadn't been for the threat that Cuspidor was posing, Holly would have felt utterly carefree.

The following weekend, Holly practiced creating a flowerpot again but with little success. She wondered why she was able to activate the brush when she least expected it. Most of the time it didn't work, and she was frustrated.

Her failure turned the weekend into a discouraging time. But before she realized it, Monday morning had arrived and now Holly had mixed feelings about going to school. She was excited to learn something she had always wanted, but she was scared that she would fail.

Her schedule looked promising. It started with Creation and Deletion I, Gate Paintings I, and Unfinished Painting I. In the afternoon, she had Projectile Brushstrokes I and a few other classes. Holly didn't know what it all meant, but even though it sounded interesting, she was quite concerned that she would end up being the laughingstock of the school if she couldn't activate the brush again.

When they arrived at Cliffony, Ileana was already waiting for them. She led them through the maze of hallways until they arrived at the Veronese Green Room. Professor Lapia was already waiting for them.

"Oh no, look who's here," Amanda said. "They are so annoying."

Gina and Lismahoon were sitting in the front row. Not wanting a confrontation, Holly steered Amanda to the other side of the room and sat down.

"Welcome students. For those who don't know me yet, I'm Lilly Lapia, and I will introduce you to the basics of painting."

Lapia adjusted her pink wig. "Creation and Deletion are two of the pillars of painting. We will start with very simple brushstrokes today. Please take out your paintbrushes. We will be creating a stone."

The professor pointed the brush at her desk. "You have to see the image of the stone clearly before your eyes." She closed her eyes and swung her brush. "The clearer your visualization, the clearer your stone will be. Then, focus on the brush and make one circle in the air."

Lapia drew a circle. Sparks shot out from her brush, paint followed, and a bright red pebble formed on her desk.

"Now you try it," she said to the class.

Everybody waved their brushes in the air. Gray rocks of all sizes popped up all over the classroom. A few students painted huge boulders, while others created precious gems. A miniature slate mountain shot up in front of Lapia and blocked her from view, while Gina painted a hailstorm of pebbles that purposely rained down on Amanda, who was noticeably annoyed about it. Serafina Abby's brush went out of control, and dozens of stalagmites and stalactites grew from the ground and ceiling, turning the classroom into a cavern. The whole place quickly became a mess.

Holly swung her brush wildly. Up and down, back and forth, round and round—but not a single spark came out. She clenched her fist and slapped the brush down on the desk in frustration. It had worked so well at the exam, and now she was right back to where she had started. She knew she had done it before and Gullveig had told her what to do, but it just wasn't working.

"Don't worry," said Lapia as she picked up Holly's brush and handed it back to her. "It is like learning to ride a bicycle. One moment you fall and the next you are zooming down the street. It takes a while until you have figured it out, but once you know how it works, you will never forget how to do it." Lapia walked back to her desk.

Holly sat down. Maybe she was impatient and expected too much from herself. Maybe over time she would learn how to focus on what the instructors expected from her and at the same moment have the desire to do it.

While Holly was still wondering about how she would find her talent, Gina came over, holding a gem in her palm. "I guess we're not as good as we pretend to be, are we, Gindar?" she hissed and then laughed out loud.

Professor Lapia backed away from her desk, which had been lifted up to the ceiling by a giant stalagmite. "That's enough, kids," she hollered. "Please stop."

Everyone sat down. The professor helped a few students to dissolve their creations.

"Let's try something lighter," she said. "Something less dangerous. Maybe a feather."

Once she had demonstrated the correct brushstroke, the chaos started all over again. A cloud of feathers rained down on the class, covering the professor in a mountain of fluff.

Holly glanced enviously at the feathers the students had created. She could swing the brush back and forth, make the circle small or large—but nothing came out of it. While Holly hammered the brush against her desk to see if she could at least get something out of it, Lapia rushed over to Serafina, who had accidentally grown an ostrich feather on her behind.

"Oh my dear, what did you do there?" said Lapia, examining the girl's backside. "I will have to take you to Professor Kaplin to fix this."

The bell rang. The class darted out of the feather-filled classroom, leaving Lapia behind in a state of complete exhaustion.

Holly was following her fellow students down Pastel Hallway when she heard Cuspidor's voice again.

"Holly!" Cuspidor boomed from one of the hallways. "My plan will bring you to me."

"What plan?" Holly asked.

But Cuspidor did not respond. Instead, a boy a head shorter than her looked at her, confused.

"Are you talking to yourself?" the boy asked.

"Forget it," Holly said and left her fellow students. She followed the hallway where the voice had come from until she reached the Gallery of Wonders again.

The sphinx opened one eye and growled, "Ah, you again. What do you want this time?"

"Nothing, I was just passing by," said Holly.

The sphinx furrowed his brows skeptically.

"I'm late," said Holly as bell rang through the hallway. "Gate Paintings I in the Madder Pink Room. Do you know where that is?"

"Down that way," said the sphinx, pointing in the opposite direction from which Holly had come.

Holly raced down the hallway. Out of breath, she finally stumbled into the right classroom.

"Late on the first day," said the instructor, while writing something on the blackboard. "Not a good start."

Holly froze in place as the instructor turned around. It was Ms. Hubbleworth with that nasty macaw on her sunhat. Holly sat down next to Rufus.

"Where were you?" Rufus asked.

"I just got lost," whispered Holly. "What is Ms. Hubbleworth doing here?"

"I have no idea, but she seems pretty in tune with her new job," Rufus said.

"I think this is really strange," Holly said. "Our first day in Magora, she kept shouting that she wasn't a professor."

Ms. Hubbleworth put her hands on her hips, cleared her throat, and introduced herself to the class. "I'm your professor for Gate Painting I. As you know, the Gallery of Wonders is being renovated. Since all gate paintings are located in the Gallery of Wonders, there is nothing for me to do this year."

"Why is the Gallery of Wonders being renovated?" Gina asked. "It didn't look as if it needed a new coat of paint last time I was in there."

"Why don't they move the paintings to another room so we can use them?" a Ledesma boy in the back row asked.

"Is there a problem with the Gallery?" Brian asked. "Could it be that the Duke of—"

Professor Hubbleworth whipped around and hushed Brian. "This has nothing to do with Cuspidor. The Gallery needs a new coat of paint. There is no problem whatsoever." Her beehive was shaking. She sat down in her chair.

"Next week, a substitute will take over," she said. "Professor LePawnee and I have agreed that my experience is more needed elsewhere until I can resume with the original curriculum. Unfortunately, Professor Winney has an ear infection this week but from next week on, he will take over."

Holly thought that Ms. Hubbleworth had reacted rather strangely. If there was no problem with the gallery, why would the giant sphinx be in front of the entrance? Did it have anything to do with Holly hearing Cuspidor's voice in the gallery? Holly had a feeling that he was in there, and the school was trying to keep him locked in by placing the sphinx in front of the door.

Ms. Hubbleworth took off her sunhat, distributed some handouts about the history of gate paintings, and disappeared behind a newspaper called *The Magoran Times*. For the remaining time, Holly pretended to read the handouts, but her mind was focused on the Gallery of Wonders.

"I have to talk to Ms. Hubbleworth," Holly whispered to Brian. "I want to know why she's acting as though she has always taught here. I wonder what happened after she took the MSP."

Eventually, the bell rang, and the students scurried out of the classroom. Holly walked to the professor's desk and leaned over. "Did you have any difficulties after taking the MSP?"

"Pardon me?" Ms. Hubbleworth asked.

Holly repeated her question, but her nosy neighbor from Donkleywood stared at her with a confused look on her face.

Holly was a bit irritated, but then she realized—Ms. Hubbleworth was trying to cover up that she was not really from Magora. She was just pretending to be a professor, trying to hide her real identity as someone from Donkleywood in order not to be seen as an imposter.

"You really have played your role well," said Holly. "Nobody around here has noticed. You can stop your charade now."

"Child, what on earth are you talking about?" Ms. Hubbleworth asked.

"Donkleywood and the Smoralls. Remember? You pulled me up by my ear." Holly threw a few words at her, trying to make her remember.

"Stop this nonsense," scolded Ms. Hubbleworth, her voice rising. "I have been an instructor at Cliffony for years, and I have never, ever pulled a child by the ear."

"All right, tell me how you made them believe you're an instructor," said Holly. It was impossible that her Donkleywood neighbor had forgotten all about her past—or had she suffered some kind of brain damage because of the MSP?

Ms. Hubbleworth jumped up, knocking her chair over backward. "Enough is enough. Nobody doubts my ability as

an instructor."

She pushed Holly out of the room and slammed the door shut.

"I read in the *Encyclopedia of Magora* that MSP sometimes clouds your mind for months," said Rufus, who had overheard the conversation. "She might still be suffering from the aftereffects."

"I was thinking that as well," said Holly. "It must be amnesia, so she doesn't remember anything."

The following weeks passed without any major occurrences except that Ms. Hubbleworth did not show up for class anymore. As promised, she had sent for Professor Winney, an old faun, as a substitute, who made them copy passages from textbooks. It turned out to be the most boring class of the school year.

Rufus had been given permission to spend the class period in the library. He was reading everything he could to find another way back to Donkleywood, while Amanda utilized the time to fix her nails and work on her makeup.

Holly and Brian enjoyed practicing brushstrokes and walking around the griffin hatchery.

Aside from Gate Paintings I, most classes were a lot of fun. As a matter of fact, Holly loved Cliffony so much that her desire to return to Donkleywood would have faded if she hadn't told herself repeatedly that she was just living in a painting. But life in Magora was so much better than in Donkleywood that Holly was beginning to feel at home.

Everything would have been perfect if it hadn't been for the constant echo of Cuspidor's voice. Holly felt the day was coming very soon when she would find out what Cuspidor wanted from her.

Professor Farouche's Class

Losing the line is a danger because when fantasy and reality become one, we have no contrast. Without contrast, a world becomes dull and boring.

The days grew shorter as the cold crept into the classrooms of Cliffony. The red shingles on the houses around the academy were covered in snow. Papplewick Street had turned into an ice slide, and the students enjoyed scooting down on sleighs, boards, and boxes.

Holly kept practicing her brushstrokes, hoping that one day she would get a spark out of the brush. Even though she wasn't successful, she loved Cliffony and being with her friends—if only Cuspidor's voice didn't keep echoing in her mind.

Amanda had begun to make jokes about Holly hearing voices, so Holly had decided not to fan those flames anymore, and she began to act as if she no longer heard Cuspidor.

Classes continued without interruption, and Holly enjoyed most of them. Only one class turned out to be a total nightmare: Unfinished Painting I. Professor Farouche was grumpy and unfriendly all the time, and he rarely gave good grades to anyone.

One afternoon, Holly arrived late for Farouche's class. She had picked up Tenshi during lunch to show him to some of her fellow students. As she opened the heavy iron door in the basement of the castle where Farouche had set up his classroom, a shrill scream penetrated her ears. Tenshi flinched and crawled into Holly's backpack. A few candles lit the dark cellar. Holly could see that Farouche had tied a rabbit to his desk. Squealing, the rabbit jerked back and forth, trying to pull off its iron muzzle.

Farouche's eyes turned into two glowing slits. "Our little Gindar gives us the honor of coming to class."

"I'm really sorry to be late. I—"

"Quiet, O'Flanigan, and come here," Farouche snapped.

As Holly stepped closer, she noticed that the creature on the desk was not a rabbit. From the neck up, it looked like a rabbit, but from the head down, it was nothing but a drawing. Pencil lines hovered in the air, outlining the lower body. Between the lines was nothing but air.

"You have never seen an Unfinished, have you?" Farouche asked.

"No, I haven't," mumbled Holly, her eyes fixed hypnotically on the pencil lines. It was fascinating to watch them move rapidly in the air without changing the overall shape of the

creature.

"The Unfinished are the most dangerous creatures you can encounter," said Farouche. "Today I'll show you how to protect yourselves from an Unfinished. I need a volunteer for this experiment."

Some students slid down in their chairs to get out of Farouche's sight.

"Don't worry. I will be practicing on a Nukimai first, not on any of you—yet."

Holly's heart began to race as Tenshi began to squeal. She was afraid that the professor might find Tenshi and use him for his experiment. Holly opened her backpack and pressed her hand over his mouth to quiet him.

"Let's start the experiment," Farouche said as he pulled out a cage from underneath one of the tables. Inside was another Nukimai about twice the size of Tenshi.

Relieved, Holly let go of Tenshi's mouth, and he quiet down.

Farouche unfastened the muzzle on the Unfinished. The other Nukimai whined loudly as Farouche tightened him to a brick.

"The Unfinished need a large amount of blood to become a complete painting," explained Farouche. "They are very fragile and need a finished coat for protection, just as any normal painting does. Sunlight can dissolve them—that's why the Unfinished avoid sunlight."

Farouche moved the brick with the Nukimai closer to the rabbit. The Nukimai threw his head from one side to the other, desperately trying to break free.

"Stop it," Holly shouted as the class murmured. "You're hurting him."

"Be quiet," Farouche said. "Don't interrupt this experiment. The Nukimai will be fine."

Holly could not bear to watch how the Nukimai struggled. She covered her face with her hands.

"Unfinished animals are very easy to feed," continued Farouche. "They take any kind of blood. Unfinished humans are more selective."

Holly looked between her fingers at Farouche. He was grinning at Ileana, who had been very quiet ever since the experiment had started. Now tears began rolling down her cheeks.

"I think Ms. Kennicott can tell us a little more about what nasty and evil creatures the Unfinished are," Farouche said.

Ileana covered her face, started sobbing, and ran out of the classroom. Holly wanted to go after her, but Farouche's look clearly indicated that she had better stay and be quiet.

"They should be expelled from Cliffony," said Gina. "Unfinished are scum."

Holly clenched her fists and was about to jump at Gina when Farouche held her back.

"No fighting in my classroom," he said. "Let's continue. As I was saying, unfinished humans cannot use animal blood. Ordinary Unfinished can take any human blood, like that of Tracers. But Legumers need Legumer blood."

"What about Gindars?" Rufus asked.

"Gindar blood is the most valuable. Everybody can use it: animals, humans, Tracers, and Legumers."

"So an unfinished Gindar could only be completed by using Gindar blood," Gina said.

"Correct," said Farouche. "But there are no unfinished Gindars. If a Gindar painted another Gindar, he would never leave him unfinished. Gindars are too important. Now let's see what will happen when an Unfinished attacks its prey."

Farouche pushed the brick with the Nukimai closer to the Unfinished. Holly wanted to scream, but instead she bit her lower lip. Then she saw the rabbit bury his teeth deep into the Nukimai's neck. The Nukimai screeched.

When Holly saw that, she could no longer hold back. "Stop it! You'll kill him," she yelled, jumping forward.

Farouche stopped Holly and pushed her back into the crowd of students. "You are becoming a little pest," he said. "Back off. I told you he'll be all right. Don't interrupt this experiment again."

"I would be quiet now if I were you," whispered Rufus. "He might give you detention."

Professor Farouche turned back to the Unfinished. "Everybody watch carefully now."

The class closed in on Farouche's desk, now both horrified and curious. The Nukimai stopped struggling and, as the rabbit sucked his blood. With every drop, the rabbit's appearance changed. The blood that had entered the rabbit turned into paint and whirled around. Slowly, the paint changed into flesh. It was like pouring milk into an empty glass.

"The pencil lines are filling up," explained Farouche. "But we are not going to finish the rabbit today. It takes many creatures' blood to complete an Unfinished."

When the belly of the rabbit was almost completed, Farouche lifted his brush and made two strokes. A thread of white paint shot out and hit the rabbit on the back. It screeched twice and let go of the Nukimai. The rabbit fell unconscious.

Holly sped forward, untied the Nukimai, and checked to see if he was fine. Tenshi gave a brief grunt in the backpack.

"I don't know why you are so worried about a Nukimai," Professor Farouche said. "It only lost a little blood, so it will be all right," He lifted him up by the collar and sat him back in the cage. "This rabbit could have drained the Nukimai completely if I hadn't stopped it. Remember, this can happen to you." He pointed his brush at Serafina Abby, whose lollipop once again dropped right out of her mouth. "The Unfinished will destroy you unless you learn how to protect yourself."

"How do we do that?" Gina asked.

"Everybody back to their seats now," said Farouche. "We do that by using our magic brushes. The brushstroke is simple: two lines crossed. But, that's not all. You need a lot of strength to ward off an Unfinished—inner strength."

Farouche lifted the rabbit over his head. "This rabbit will be a complete painting by the end of this year. Each of you will practice on him until you know how to protect yourselves." He dropped the rabbit into an iron container, thrust the door shut, and paced up and down along the first row. "In a fight with an Unfinished you can lose a lot of blood, fall unconscious, or even die. I will teach you how to protect yourselves. The key is to be prepared."

Farouche stopped abruptly in front of Holly's desk and leaned forward. "Let's practice now. Since you felt so much for this Nukimai I think it would be good if you found out for yourself what it's like to be drained by an Unfinished."

Holly's heart sank. This is what she got for drawing too much attention to herself by trying to help that Nukimai.

Gina, Lismahoon, and a few other students cheered loudly.

"See? Everybody wants you to show how good of a Gindar you are," Farouche said.

Holly did not want to go through the same thing that the Nukimai had endured but she also didn't want to look like a coward. Reluctantly, she trudged to the front.

"Once the rabbit has bitten you, make the brushstrokes," Farouche said.

Holly wondered if the bite would hurt.

"Now listen carefully," said Farouche. "If you don't do as I say, your blood will flow into the rabbit. Don't let this happen. If you don't have any confidence in yourself, the Unfinished will take advantage of you. He will enter your mind and try to distract you until you are too weak to fight."

Holly gulped, glancing back at Brian who gave her two thumbs up. Farouche woke the rabbit, unlatched the door of the iron container, and held it at arm's length. Unwillingly, Holly placed her index finger in the container. Pain shot up her arm as the rabbit buried his teeth into her flesh. The vault became blurred and everything around her slowed down.

The Unfinished

Fantasy can become dull, and we lose the magic.

You doubt that you are a Gindar, don't you? Holly could hear the Unfinished talking in a soft, comforting voice. *You think that your paintings aren't good enough.*

No, they are not. It was pure luck that I created that flowerpot-Nukimai.

For a moment, Holly hesitated. She had said something without even moving her lips. She realized the Unfinished was speaking directly to her mind.

You are afraid of being a Gindar. You are afraid of being responsible for Magora's destiny.

The Unfinished said aloud what Holly had never realized—being a Gindar did mean that Magora's very survival depended on her. Did she want to be weighed down with such an enormous burden?

"Holly, don't give up," came Brian's voice from a distance. Why was he shouting?

Don't listen to him, said the Unfinished.

"Holly! Fight," Amanda's voice sounded from somewhere distant. "The Unfinished is distracting you."

Holly remembered what Farouche had said. The Unfinished would try to demoralize her until she was too weak to fight. She focused on Brian's voice. How small were her fears compared to the bliss of having Brian, Rufus, Ileana, and even Amanda around?

With an effort, Holly's swung her arm upward and drew an "X" in the air.

The gentle voice of the Unfinished turned into a shrill scream, and it released Holly's finger.

While the class applauded, Holly sat down, nauseated. She noticed that the hind leg of the Unfinished had been partially completed.

"Not bad," admitted Farouche reluctantly. "But next time won't be so easy."

"Can I leave now?" Holly asked. She felt a boost of self-confidence. She had won against an Unfinished. "I think I have done enough for today."

"Go," Farouche said, pointing at the door.

Holly grabbed her backpack with Tenshi inside and left the classroom. As she turned the corner, she found Ileana sitting on the stairs leading up to the ground floor. She was still crying.

Holly sat down next to Ileana and put her arm around her.

"They don't know what an Unfinished has to go through," said Ileana. "You don't want to hurt anybody, but there is this voice deep inside you. It tells you to find blood and do anything for it—even kill."

"You are no longer an Unfinished," said Holly. "Farouche is wrong to treat you as one." She jumped up from the stairs. "Let's get out of here."

A smile crossed Ileana's face and she wiped away her tears. "Thanks, Holly. You are such a good friend."

At that moment, the bell rang and Rufus, Brian, and Amanda came out.

"Are you all right?" Brian asked Holly. "I can't believe that Farouche did that."

"What a nasty freak," Amanda said.

"I'm fine," Holly said. "We are both fine." She took Ileana's hand and squeezed it.

"How did it feel when the Unfinished drained your blood?" Rufus asked.

"It was strange," said Holly. "I heard the Unfinished talking to me."

"But it was a good lesson," Rufus said. "This way we will learn how to protect ourselves from the Unfinished."

"We should practice the protection brushstroke until next week," Brian said.

"Then let us get started," Rufus said.

The following week, none of the students seemed to be able to rid themselves of the rabbit except Holly, and after a while the rabbit was completed.

Holly was proud that she could do something others couldn't do, but Gina still managed to put a damper on her confidence.

"You haven't practiced on unfinished humans," Gina said, hissing. "They are much more dangerous. Professor Farouche doesn't let students practice on them until second year."

A few days later, after Creation and Deletion I, Professor Lapia called Holly and her friends to her office. Holly had been at Cliffony for almost three months now, yet she was still unable to create an object. Maybe she was about to get a warning because of that. But then why would the professor want her friends to join them? Professor Lapia led them through a back door down to her office. The spacious room was adorned with golden-framed oil paintings, and hundreds of books sat on mahogany shelves. It looked like an ancient library.

To Holly's surprise, LePawnee and Farouche were sitting in two of the four leather wing chairs.

Professor LePawnee got up as Holly stepped into the office with her friends by her side.

"Rumors are circulating that you've been hearing a voice," LePawnee said.

"Oh, that's what this is about?" Holly asked. "The voice is gone now." She thought it was better to keep it to herself that she still heard Cuspidor. She didn't want to be considered a nutcase, let alone be expelled for being mentally unfit. "I only heard it once."

Holly glanced at Rufus, knowing that he jotted down each time she had heard Cuspidor. But Rufus kept silent. Instead of paying attention, he walked to the end of the room toward a painting.

"She's lying," accused Farouche.

"Mortimor, when Holly says the voice is gone, it is gone," said LePawnee. "You see, Holly, we assume it is Cuspidor who is trying to contact you."

Professor Lapia suddenly leaped toward Rufus. He was staring at an oil painting of an Asian landscape in a niche of the office. Lapia grabbed him by the shoulders and pushed him gently back into the center of the room. For a moment, Holly wondered why Rufus was paying attention to something else when he was usually so focused.

"Is everything all right, Lilly?" LePawnee asked.

"Yes, of course," said Lapia. "I'm sorry for the interruption. I don't like people wandering around my office."

"Are you saying that Cuspidor was communicating with Holly?" Brian asked.

"Yes, very likely," said LePawnee. "We think that Cuspidor is a Gindar and that he's after her. A new Gindar poses a great threat to him. Magora could become powerful again."

"How come we cannot hear that voice?" Rufus asked.

"Gindars share a mental connection that others don't," explained Professor LePawnee. "I don't know how it works, but it's like telepathy. Maybe Holly has locked into his thoughts." She opened the door and motioned for them to leave. "I want all of you to watch out for her." She pointed at Holly's friends, who nodded solemnly.

They left the office in silence. Holly felt queasy after hearing the threat she was under, but she felt even worse that she had lied to Professor LePawnee. Despite the fact that the conversation hadn't been about grades, Holly studied harder than ever for the next few days. She wanted to learn the brushstrokes that would protect her in case Cuspidor ever attacked her.

A few days later, Holly had Projectile Brushstrokes, which was a class on how to move objects. Professor Gobeli had gathered her students in Cliffony's snow-covered courtyard. Earlier in the year, Holly had learned to move small objects around, but the professor had announced last week that they would continue with more complicated brushstrokes.

"Today we'll try the Cannon Brushstroke," announced Gobeli. "This is one of the most powerful and destructive among all projectiles."

Holly shuffled through the snow, wearing two padded jackets and two scarves. She could hardly move, but it was better than freezing to death in a Magorian snowstorm. The students lined up in front of a giant rock that Gobeli had created. It was the size of a house.

"The brushstroke—circle-dash-circle-cross-dash—cuts a cannonball out of the rock and shoots it toward an object," explained Gobeli. "Concentrate on the movement of the stone, not the stone itself."

"I'm freezing to death," whispered Holly. "Let's hurry up and get it over with."

"Looks like a difficult brushstroke to me," said Brian. "I don't think we'll be done that fast."

The professor pulled her knitted cap down over her ears and threw her braids over her shoulders. "This is not a creation class, so I don't care what the cannonball looks like. I want you to move it. Now, each of you, shoot your cannonball at the Tower of Bats."

Dark gray paint shot out of Rufus' brush and encircled the rock. The paint carved out some pebbles and shot them right at the Tower of Bats.

"That's a good start, Mr. Letterhead," said Gobeli. "When each of you has done at least as much as Mr. Letterhead, we can return to the classroom." The professor spread the students around the rock so that each of them could practice. "Anybody who carves a stone larger than a pebble won't get homework for two weeks." Gobeli beamed.

"She is only grinning so confidently because she knows that first-year students can't carve anything but pebbles," said Ileana, grumbling.

"I want to get out of here," said Holly. "My ears are so frozen they're about to fall off."

"If you want to get out of here, you had better start practicing," Rufus said.

Holly swung the brush with ease. There was no pressure on her to create anything. She only had to carve a rock. Paint shot from her brush.

Gobeli's jaw dropped as Holly carved a six-foot boulder out of the rock. The giant cannonball spun around a dozen times, shot up in the air, and sped toward the Tower of Bats.

The professor's confident smile vanished in an instant.

"Oh no. Please, you can't d-d-do that," she stuttered, darting through the snow.

Surrounded by her bats, she threw herself between the cannonball and the Tower. "You are not going to destroy my tower," she shouted, holding out her brush. But the cannonball was too fast. It whizzed by, taking a few of Gobeli's bats with it. The professor barely reached the safety of a snow hill before Holly's boulder hit the tower. The ground shook, the wall gave in, and an avalanche of rocks rained down into the courtyard. A gigantic hole gaped from the tower's fifteenth floor.

With her braids twisted around her neck, the professor stumbled out of the snow hill and tried her best to compose herself. "That was impressive. How did you do that?" she asked.

"I just wanted to get it over with," said Holly, staring flabbergasted at the hole.

"If these aren't Gindar powers, I don't know what are," said Gobeli, trying to untangle her snow-covered braids.

Holly was happy she had found something that she was extremely good at, even though she doubted that carving a rock was equally as powerful as creating a living being. And that was what a Gindar was good at.

"We'd better go back inside and practice on something lighter," Gobeli said, and she ushered them all back to the classroom.

The Ward

Sharp lines are for realistic minds.

On the day before Christmas Eve, Holly and Brian waited for Rufus at the magic bookstore. Rufus wanted to get a book on Southeast Asia. He left the store carrying a massive volume with a silk lining.

"*Asian Languages and Their Distribution*," Holly read the title on the cover.

"What do you need that for?" Brian asked, wrapping his scarf tighter around his neck. "You're just too brainy sometimes, Rufus."

Rufus flipped through the pages. "You do not understand. This could be of utmost importance."

"Whatever," Brian said, rolling his eyes.

A moment later, Brian tapped Holly on the shoulder.

"Look. The giant is gone," he said, pointing down at the corner of Ravenscraig Lane and Papplewick Street.

They walked over to the narrow alley where they met up with Ileana and Amanda. Rufus followed.

"Oh no—you do not want to go in there," Rufus said.

"We'll just take a quick peek around the corner where Ravenscraig Lane turns," Holly replied. "I want to see what's behind there."

"It is forbidden to enter without a password," Ileana said. "And I'm sure the giant will be back soon."

"Come on, Ileana," said Brian. "We might never get the chance again."

"All right," Ileana said reluctantly as she followed Holly.

Brian grabbed Rufus' arm and dragged him unwillingly down Ravenscraig Lane. Holly and Amanda headed to the corner. The buildings along the way leaned menacingly toward the street, causing the roofs to almost touch each other. Neither sunlight nor snow could fall between the rundown buildings.

"It's not a good idea to come here," Rufus whispered.

"Don't be such a chicken," said Holly. "We'll just go and see what's behind there."

She peeked around the corner, expecting nothing but a continuation of the street. To her surprise, however, the street was bustling with people. They were wearing black cloaks and hoods as if they didn't want to be recognized. In each building along the street was a rundown store. Holly looked across the street into the window of a shop just a few feet away from her. It offered black canvases, brushes with evil-looking grimaces on the handles, and gloomy art supplies that were not sold in the reputable shops on Papplewick Street. A rusty sign that read "Paint & Potions" dangled above a messy display window of a nearby store. Holly left the others behind and tiptoed across the street to the window.

"Holly," whispered Rufus, looking around the corner. "Come back. Quick. You said only to the corner!"

"Don't be such a chicken," Holly said.

Brian and Ileana pointed frantically down the street. Holly turned around and saw a cloaked man headed in her direction. She gulped as she saw the man's face. It was Professor Farouche.

She scooted back and made it just in time before Farouche reached the Paint and Potions shop. He passed the display window and entered a stucco-covered building a few feet from the corner.

"What on earth is he doing here?" Brian asked.

"Let's go find out," Holly said.

"This is a not a good idea," said Rufus as he stumbled behind Holly toward the stucco building.

A sign that read "The Ward" dangled above the door. Holly pushed open the heavy iron door and stepped inside. Paintings of werewolves, vampires, and dragons covered the walls of a narrow torch-lit corridor that led into darkness. A rotten stench filled the air. Holly had to cover her nose with her scarf or she would have thrown up.

"I do not think we should be here," Rufus whispered.

Nervously, Ileana took a step back. "This time I think Rufus is right. Something isn't right about this place," she said.

"Oh come on, you guys," interrupted Brian. "You can't be

scared by a few paintings."

"That's not it," replied Ileana. "I don't like the smell of dead flesh."

"Eww," Amanda said.

"Is that dead flesh?" Rufus cried, tumbling backward out the door.

"I remember this smell from the time when I was an Unfinished," said Ileana. "It's carrion. The Unfinished suck people's blood until they are dead and then they let them rot."

"Maybe there is just a meat market down there," Holly said, even though she doubted it herself. But she wanted to make Rufus feel more comfortable.

Ileana backed out of the corridor. "I'll wait outside," she said. "Please be careful."

Rufus nodded and followed Ileana outside.

Holly was now more curious than ever. She wanted to find out what was at the end of the corridor. She left Ileana behind and walked into darkness, followed by Brian and Amanda. After a few minutes, she reached a large marble hall that looked like the nave of a cathedral. It was lit by torches. Statues of dragons lined the walls, while stone gargoyles looked down from the ceiling. At the end of the hall was a marble desk. It blocked the entrance to a second corridor. A pale man with a thin, black moustache and a hunchback was sitting behind the desk, talking to Farouche. Holly tiptoed closer under the cover of the statues.

"I need another Unfinished," said Farouche. "My class has almost completed the rabbit."

"A very ambitious class. Pick any you like, Mortimor," said

the pale man, pointing down the corridor.

Holly, Brian, and Amanda snuck past the pale man and followed Farouche. The corridor led to an area that looked like the entrance of a maximum-security prison. The stench of rotten meat intensified as Farouche opened the heavy gate. A dungeon with dozens of cells lined the corridor. Screams and growls echoed throughout.

Farouche walked inside and disappeared in the darkness.

Holly came out of hiding and peeked into one of the cells. Water dripped from the ceiling, creating puddles of mud on the earthen floor. A boy cowered in the farthest corner of the cell. He was tied to a pillar with a heavy chain.

"That's horrible," Holly whispered. "Why did they chain you?"

The boy glared at her. He growled like a lion as he leaped forward but the chain jerked him back like a yo-yo.

Holly picked up one of the torches that lined the corridor. As the light flickered, she took a closer look through the rusty bars, and understood. This was not a boy—it was an Unfinished. The boy's head was complete, while the rest of the body was nothing but pencil lines.

"Look at them. How creepy," Amanda said, pointing at another cell, where three women with unfinished heads lay on the ground. Dried-up pieces of meat were scattered around them. It looked as if they were fed like animals in a cage.

"The Ward is a prison for the Unfinished," said Holly, horrified. "Why can't Gindars finish their tasks? If I ever become a Gindar, I will finish everything I start."

As Holly watched an unfinished girl without legs crawl

along the barren mud floor, Farouche reappeared at the far end of the corridor.

"Watch out," whispered Amanda, darting into a niche between two cells.

Brian and Holly sped after Amanda and hid until Farouche had passed with a cage containing an ermine.

"That must be the next Unfinished we'll practice on," Brian whispered.

"Let's go back now," Holly said.

They snuck through the marble hall past the hunchback and reached Ravenscraig Lane a few moments later.

"Over here," Rufus whispered.

He was hiding with Ileana behind the door of the ward.

"That was close," said Ileana. "Farouche almost saw us when he came out, but we were able to jump behind a garbage can."

"What happened in there?" Rufus asked.

Holly pulled him to the side and told him what they had seen. She didn't want Ileana to know that Unfinished were kept under these conditions.

"Look, Farouche is going into the Paint and Potions shop," Amanda said.

"Let's follow him," Brian said. "I think he's up to no good."

"Have you not had enough?" Rufus asked.

"I don't trust Farouche," said Holly. "I have a feeling he has something to hide."

She squeezed through the slightly open door of the Paint and Potions shop, knowing that any sudden movement might

set off the bell. Reluctantly, Rufus and the others followed. Once they were all inside, they hid behind large barrels and a few shelves that were crammed with ink bottles of all shapes, sizes, and colors. A coat of dust covered every inch of the store, including the dozens of spider webs that hung between the bottles.

Farouche was standing behind the counter, talking to a creature that was about three feet tall. Holly crawled on all fours to get a better look at the creature. His head was disproportionately large, and his skin was completely wrinkled. His tiny red eyes were deeply set. It was nauseating to watch the dozens of warts on his giant nose ooze with pus.

"Not even the best cucumber mask could fix his complexion," Amanda whispered.

Brian took a deep breath and rolled his eyes. "Amanda, that's a leprechaun."

"He still needs a good face peel," Amanda said.

Brian ground his teeth and whispered to Holly, "I think blonde jokes have their justification."

Farouche handed the unfinished ermine to the leprechaun, who locked it in a barrel and trudged into another room. Farouche opened an ornate wardrobe and climbed inside. Just as the door shut behind him, Holly sprung out of her hiding place while Brian ran over to the room that the leprechaun had just entered.

"He's headed outside," Brian said, looking around the corner into the other room.

"Let's follow Farouche," Holly said.

"Oh no—we are not going in there," said Rufus, holding

on to Holly's sleeve.

But Holly dragged Rufus through the room anyway.

"You don't think Farouche would climb into a wardrobe and sit there, do you?" Holly asked. "I'm sure it's a secret entrance."

"To what?" Amanda asked.

"Let's find out," Holly said.

"Watch out. The leprechaun is coming back," Brian said as he jumped behind a barrel.

Holly opened the wardrobe, looked inside, and said, "See? Farouche is gone." Then she jumped inside, taking Rufus with her. She shut the door quietly and waited. A few minutes passed. Then the door opened, and Brian peeked inside.

"Holy smokes. That was close." Brian smiled. "The leprechaun was—" A shove from behind pushed Brian headfirst inside. Amanda and Ileana almost crushed him as they jumped into the wardrobe behind Brian.

"Close the door quickly," said Ileana. "The leprechaun is back again."

Holly wedged in toward the back of the wardrobe. As her face pressed against the rough back paneling, she felt something cold on her arm. She touched the object and realized it was a door knob. She turned it gently, and the back paneling slid to the side.

"I knew it," she whispered. "The wardrobe has a secret door."

A small tunnel led into darkness.

The Secret Tunnel

Sharp lines separate fantasy and reality completely. People with sharp lines in their minds sort all events, persons, actions, or places into either reality or fantasy. They will never experience the magic that people with blurry lines see on an everyday basis.

Holly crawled through the tunnel until she reached a large pet door at the end. She pushed it open and found herself in a lush garden. There was no sign of snow, and the flowers were in full bloom. Exotic plants of all sizes lined a path that wound through a tropical landscape.

"Holy smokes," Brian said when he came out of the tunnel. "Where are we?"

"Look, that is why there is no snow," said Rufus, pointing at a huge glass dome above. "It is a greenhouse."

"Let's find Farouche," said Holly. "He must be somewhere around here."

She followed the curved trail, passing a few orchids the size of pumpkins, until she reached a steep cliff with two cave entrances.

"Gors," Rufus cried as he froze on the spot.

Four Gors protected the two entrances, two by each cave, holding sharp swords in their hands. Beyond each entrance was a staircase, one going up, the other leading down.

"Let us go back. We cannot pass the Gors," said Rufus, clearly relieved.

"Oh, yes we can," said Holly. From her backpack, she pulled out the jar with MSP and grinned at Rufus. "Should we go up or down?"

"You know well enough that we are not supposed to use MSP," Rufus said. "Remember how long it took us to recover?"

"But we know how to use it now," said Holly, ignoring Rufus' advice. She sprinkled a bit of MSP over her head and handed it to Brian. He also used it. A minute later, Holly felt her mind flying high above. She passed the Gors without a problem and focused on her body that walked below. This time, her mind was reunited with her body without complications.

"It worked," shouted Holly. "Come on, you guys." She waved to the others.

"It's much easier the second time," Brian said after his mind had reunited with his body.

Ileana shied away as Amanda handed her the jar. "I can't take that," she said. "I was an Unfinished. If I take MSP, my mind will dissolve, just as an Unfinished will fade away if exposed to sunlight."

"But you're not an Unfinished anymore," Amanda said.

"But I was recently completed," explained Ileana. "In a year or so I might be okay, but now it is too dangerous. It's all right, you go on without me."

Rufus and Amanda sprinkled the MSP over their heads and joined Holly and Brian behind the Gors. Ileana waited in the garden.

"We'll be back," Holly called out. "If we are not back in an hour, get some help." They climbed the staircase that led into darkness, leaving Ileana behind. When she looked back down, Holly only saw a silhouette in a dot of light.

She puffed and stopped. Was this staircase ever going to end?

"Holly. I need you," Cuspidor boomed.

Holly twitched. "I'm hearing Cuspidor again," she whispered.

"Do you think he's close by?" Brian asked.

Holly shrugged while Rufus climbed a few more steps until he was a head taller than everyone else. He put his hands on his hips and admonished, "I told you this was not a good idea. Do you think they placed the Gors there just for fun?"

"Rufus is right," said Brian. "They wouldn't have placed Gors at the entrance if Cuspidor wasn't around. Only Gors can keep Cuspidor out."

"Or a sphinx," Rufus said.

"What do you mean?" asked Holly.

Rufus replied, "I have read in the encyclopedia that Cuspidor tried to break into Cliffony many years ago. A professor found out that a sphinx fought him off."

"So the sphinx in Cliffony is not to keep the students out of the Gallery of Wonders, but to keep Cuspidor out of Cliffony," Holly said. "That's just what I suspected."

"I think we had better go back," Rufus said.

"I can't run away from Cuspidor forever," said Holly. "I'll have to face him sooner or later and find out what he wants. Otherwise, I'll never get his voice out of my mind."

She pressed her hands against her head to silence the murmur she was hearing. "Let's go on."

After a few more steps, the staircase turned into a tunnel that led deeper into the cliff. They tiptoed through the tunnel until it opened up to a magnificent round hall. Niches with marble statues of men who looked like kings lined the walls. An intricate mosaic of an orchid surrounded by butterflies decorated the entire floor.

"This looks like a hall in ancient Rome," Rufus said.

"Isn't he handsome?" said Amanda, pointing at a statue of a discus thrower with a perfectly chiseled physique.

"First a professor and now a marble statue," said Brian, rolling his eyes again.

"Better look at that," said Rufus, pointing ahead of them. "It looks as if there is trouble ahead."

In the middle of the marble wall was a hole as big as a garage door. Rubble piled up in front of it. A path had been cleared through the rubble, leading to the opposite wall. Two doors were located there. One was protected by a stone sphinx where butterflies hovered around. The other had been smashed. The

wooden planks lay scattered around.

"It looks as if someone broke through the wall, made his way to the door, and smashed it," Holly said.

"Or the other way around," Amanda said.

"Then there must be something very important in one of these places," Brian said. "Or why would you go through so much effort to break through a wall?"

Brian and Rufus climbed over the rubble and moved some of the planks of the broken door aside. Rufus peeked into the entrance. He turned around immediately with a startled look on his face.

"What's in there?" Holly asked.

But before he could answer, she heard Cuspidor's voice again, louder than ever before. She pressed both her hands against her temples and shook her head back and forth.

"Stop it, Cuspidor," she said as she turned around. "The voice is coming from there." Holly pointed at the hole in the marble wall.

Amanda ran to the hole, picked up a stone, and threw it into the opening. The stone plunged deep into the tunnel. Its echo reverberated through the Roman hall. Surprisingly, the voice stopped.

"We'd better get out of here quickly," Amanda said.

Holly turned back to Rufus who was still standing in front of the entrance with a shocked look on his face.

"You will not believe this," said Rufus. "You have to come here and see for yourself."

Holly climbed over the rubble and reached the entrance.

"This must be the Gallery of Wonders," said Rufus,

pointing at dozens of empty frames. "I believe someone has stolen the paintings."

The Gallery of Wonders

The line has many looks. It can be thick or thin, colorful or dull, wavy or straight, blurry or sharp.

The hall was so high that Holly didn't know if it had a ceiling or not. Staircases crisscrossed the gallery from top to bottom. Empty golden frames were suspended from the staircases, indicating that some of the paintings must have hung in midair while others had been on the walls. A few sunbeams fell through colorful stained-glass windows, bathing the gallery in a bright light. In the center, two spiral stone staircases intertwined like a double helix. Holly guessed these allowed a visitor to reach every corner of the endless maze.

"It was a lie," said Holly. "There are no renovations taking place here."

"Maybe they're being restored," Brian suggested.

"Gate paintings do not need restoration," explained Rufus. "They are protected by a magic coat of varnish."

"What's happened is clear," said Holly. "There's a hole in the wall, this door has been broken, the paintings are gone, and I hear Cuspidor's voice louder than ever—he must have stolen the paintings."

"Quiet," said Amanda, putting her index finger on her lips. "I hear something."

Holly listened. It was the sound of footsteps coming from the double-helix staircase.

"Whoever it is, they're coming toward us," Amanda said.

Holly gripped her brush tightly as she saw a shadow gliding over the staircase. Brian and Amanda stepped back into the Roman hall and hid around the corner of the door.

"You cannot fight Cuspidor," said Rufus, pulling on Holly's sleeve like a puppy trying to save his master.

But Holly did not move. Determined, she held her brush tightly stretched out before her. "Cuspidor will find me one day, anyhow. I might as well find out what he wants from now."

"Is it not obvious?" Rufus asked. "He wants to get rid of you."

"That's what we assume," said Holly. "But we don't have any proof."

Suddenly, blood-red boots that were oddly curled at the front appeared on the staircase.

"It's not Cuspidor," whispered Holly, recognizing the strange looking boots. "It's Farouche. He's coming our way."

Holly stumbled backward into the Roman hall; Rufus and

Amanda leaped over the pile of rubble and headed back to the tunnel.

"Let's get out of here," Holly said to Brian as they stepped back into the Roman hall. "Farouche is…"

Holly never finished the sentence. She felt a sizzling breath on the back of her neck. She turned and found herself staring right into a pair of glowing red eyes.

"Run!" Brian screamed.

Without getting a closer look at what was actually staring at her, Holly staggered over the rubble toward the tunnel.

"It's the flying seahorses," Brian yelled.

They ran through the tunnel and down the stairs until they reached the Gors. The flying seahorses pursued them.

"Where's the MSP?" Holly asked, frantically. "We need to pass the Gors."

"I have it," Amanda yelled out, a few steps ahead of Holly.

Amanda took some MSP and hurled the jar over to Holly. Holly caught it, poured some powder on her fingertip, and tossed it to Brian. At that precise moment, a giant flame shot past Holly. The seahorses were spitting fire. They were just a few yards away.

Holly sprinkled the powder over her head and leaped forward into the garden. The seahorses came to an abrupt halt behind the Gors.

Holly felt her mind floating all over the place. She was jittery, and her heart was beating faster than ever. She was relieved as she spotted exotic plants around her. Then she felt as if she had been hit on the head, and her vision failed.

Holly opened her eyes. Something was different from before, but she didn't know what. She felt tiny and stiff, but could not explain that feeling. As her vision cleared, she saw nothing but a white wall and a giant brush swinging like a pendulum in front of her. Then the face of Professor Kaplin appeared, only it was ten times larger than normal.

"What's going on?" she asked.

He didn't respond. Holly wanted to turn around, but she couldn't move. She kept staring at the white wall.

"Holly, are you all right?" She heard Brian's voice, but she couldn't see him.

"What's going on?" she asked again. "I can't move."

"Professor Kaplin, please tell us what happened," Rufus' voice echoed from somewhere.

Kaplin didn't reply, but kept swinging his brush.

Then there was another familiar voice. "So how are they doing?" Ileana's face also appeared ten times larger than normal in front of Holly. "Can they see us?"

"From previous accidents, I know that they can see and hear us, but we can't hear them," replied the professor.

"Let's turn them around, so they can see themselves in the mirror," Ileana said.

Holly felt a jolt, and her sight shifted to a mirror. The painful cries of her friends sounded around her. She screamed, too.

There, in the mirror lined up beside each other, were four plants, nicely placed in clay pots. Next to a tree that was only a foot high stood a cactus, a sunflower, and a basil plant.

"I'm a tree," Holly yelled.

"And I'm a cactus," Brian said.

"We did not concentrate on our bodies, but on the plants in the garden," moaned the basil plant with the unmistakable voice of Rufus. "I told you from the beginning that MSP is dangerous—but no one listened." When he shook his leaves, Holly suddenly caught the licorice-like smell of the basil.

"But why did you concentrate on a plant?" Holly asked.

"I could ask you the same," said Rufus accusingly. "If your life is in danger, your mind does not focus well. It panics."

"True," said Brian. "I did panic."

"Look over there in the corner," said Holly, staring at four beds lined up next to each other. In each bed there was a body. Holly gulped. "That's me in the bed on the right."

"And I'm the one on the left," said Brian. "I look as if I'm dead."

Amanda's mind had ended up in a sunflower. She opened and closed her blossom rapidly. "I look like an angel," she said happily.

Brian laughed. "You're a plant, not an angel."

"Don't you think my leaves lack a little color?" Amanda asked.

"Amanda," shouted Brian, "we're stuck in plants. I don't care if you aren't colorful enough."

Amanda kept flapping her leaves and muttered indignantly, "Why am I not surprised that you don't care? How could I expect a cactus to notice?"

For two days, they tried to regain their original shape by concentrating on their bodies, but it didn't work. All Holly felt was how the water in the ground crawled up within her and nourished her without her doing anything.

"Your minds will eventually leave the plants," said Kaplin, swinging his brush back and forth in front of Holly. "The question is, when? But don't worry, you will not die. Professor LePawnee has brought some fertilizer that will keep you healthy. She got a different kind for each of you: sunflower, basil, cactus, and oak tree."

"Oak tree?" Holly looked up and down her thin trunk. She really was one. Suddenly, she had a flash of inspiration. "Jeepers, I should have thought of that. Remember Farouche was standing under the oak in Donkleywood?"

"Sure," Brian said.

"He couldn't have come through Grandpa Nikolas' painting," said Holly. "The painting was still in the chest at the time. So they must have come through another painting."

"And that gate painting was probably in the Gallery of Wonders," Rufus said.

"Of course," said Holly. "And the cloaked creature next to Farouche in Donkleywood must have been Cuspidor. They stole the paintings in the Gallery of Wonders, entered Donkleywood through a painting, and set fire that killed Grandpa Nikolas."

"But why would Cuspidor want to kill Grandpa Nikolas?" Brian asked.

"Isn't that obvious?" said Holly. "Grandpa Nikolas was a Gindar, and he could have protected Magora. Cuspidor wants to destroy the island."

All the pieces of the puzzle were slowly coming together, but where was the other gate painting that led them to Donkleywood? Why was Farouche supporting Cuspidor?

And what was Professor Farouche doing in the Gallery of Wonders?

Time Wasted

Finding the line between fantasy and reality can be an eternal search, but on the way, we might find the magic in our lives.

It took three long weeks in the infirmary before Holly's mind finally returned to her body. She and her friends had missed Christmas and Cliffony's holiday party—and worst of all, vacation was over, and she had spent it all sitting in a pot.

In mid-January, Ileana's grinning face appeared around the door frame. "Good to have you guys back," she said. "I was starting to wonder if you would miss the Quadrennial Art Competition."

Holly got up and stretched. Everything in her body hurt from lying for weeks in the bed.

Rufus rubbed his neck, while Brian stretched his feet.

"The Quadrennial what?" Amanda asked.

"The Quadrennial Art Competition," Ileana repeated. "Don't tell me you've forgotten? It's a school contest. The winner will get the title of Cliffony's Best Artist. My brother, Calvin, won the title last time." Ileana swung the door wide open. "There is someone else who wants to talk to you."

A moss-green llama with long floppy ears trotted in. With a boom, the llama disappeared in a cloud of smoke. When the fog had cleared, Holly was looking at Cookie's smiling face.

She jumped up, sped across the room, and gave him a hug.

"Good to have you back," said Cookie. "Have you talked to Professor LePawnee yet?"

"Not yet," Holly said.

"I think she was really angry when she heard you had snuck into Ravenscraig Lane. I think she—"

"Excuse me." The professor was standing in the door with a stern expression on her face. "I would like to see all four of you in my office now."

"That doesn't sound good," Brian said.

They followed LePawnee down the hallway. Holly felt horrible for having used MSP without permission. She knew they had to face the consequences now.

When they reached the office, the professor let them in. Without saying a word, she sat behind her desk.

"It was all my fault," said Brian, briskly stepping forward.

Why was Brian ready to take all the blame? Holly was puzzled. That was not right. She was the one who had suggested using MSP in the first place. If anyone should be blamed, it

would be her.

"No, Professor LePawnee," Holly said, pushing Brian aside. "It's my fault."

"No, that's not true," said Amanda. "They are only trying to protect me. I'm the one who actually wanted to go there."

"But—" Surprised, Holly stared at Amanda's grinning face.

"We're in this together, remember?" Amanda whispered.

LePawnee got up from behind her desk. Her stern expression vanished, and a smile flitted over her face.

"I'm so glad you are all right," she said. "I do not intend to punish you for sneaking into Ravenscraig Lane. You have only done what every student at Cliffony tries to do sooner or later. Curiosity is vital when learning new things."

LePawnee threw her shiny, black hair over her shoulder and walked past Holly to a tea trolley. "I never expected you to find the secret door in the closet."

"It was because of Professor Farouche," Holly said.

"Yes, I know," said LePawnee. "He was the one who found you in the garden. Your bodies were walking around in circles. Ileana helped him determine which plants your minds had entered. He potted you up and brought you to the infirmary."

Farouche had helped them? Holly was confused. Why would the professor do that if he was working together with Cuspidor?

LePawnee poured some tea and offered it to the children. Holly smelled the delicious mango flavor and took a sip.

"There is something more important I want to discuss," said the professor. "I'm told you discovered that the paintings in the Gallery of Wonders have been stolen. Cuspidor broke in and took them."

"So it really was Cuspidor," said Holly. "Why did you keep that a secret?"

"If people were to find out that all the paintings in the gallery had been stolen, panic would break out. People would realize that we are cut off from any other place."

LePawnee poured herself a cup of tea. "As you have undoubtedly noticed, Cuspidor came through the back door. When we found out the paintings had been stolen, we placed a sphinx at the entrance to keep him out of Cliffony."

"Why would you use a sphinx?" Holly asked. "Why not Gors?"

"Gors are used to protect us. They would have attracted too much attention inside Cliffony. Everyone would have known that Cuspidor was involved," said LePawnee, sipping her tea.

"How did Cuspidor know there was a back door to the gallery?" Holly asked.

"That's a good question—we don't know." The professor sighed, glancing out the window onto icy Lake Santima. She paused for a moment, sipped her tea again, and said, "A spy. He must have an accomplice here in Cliffony. Very few people know about the back door."

"Farouche," Holly and Brian said at the same time.

LePawnee smiled. "Professor Farouche is one of my most reliable instructors. I trust him fully."

Brian leaned over LePawnee's desk. "What was he doing in the Gallery then? We've seen him do bad things before, and—"

LePawnee hushed Brian with a quick hand gesture. "That's enough. Professor Farouche would never do such a thing."

"I read that Ledesma butterflies are different from regular butterflies. Is that true?" Rufus asked.

Holly was irritated that Rufus was asking such an odd question at such a crucial moment. But he winked at her briefly, and then Holly understood that he was trying to be diplomatic and calming the atmosphere by changing the subject.

LePawnee nodded as a few of her butterflies flew up, fanned their wings, and danced in circles. "Our butterflies can exchange information. Each butterfly carries a fact, an image, or an emotion to and from the Flower of Creativity."

"What's that?" Holly asked.

"Not another plant," Brian moaned. "Having been a cactus for weeks is enough for me."

"The Flower of Creativity is what you would call our common brain," explained LePawnee. "When our butterflies have collected enough information in our heads, they fly to the flower and drop it off. They pick up new information there and bring it back to us. So there is a constant exchange between us and the flower."

A batch of purple butterflies rose from the bone lotus on the professor's head and fluttered out of the window, leaving a trail of sparkles in the air.

"See, they are now taking the information about our conversation to the Flower of Creativity," she said.

"So every Ledesma knows what the other is doing?" Holly asked.

"Not everything. Our butterflies screen the information.

Otherwise, we would be overloaded by unnecessary detail. But you could say that the flower is the collective brain of the Ledesmas. If all the butterflies died, we would die, too. And if they never left our lotuses, we would never be able to share our ideas with each other."

"Where is this flower located?" Rufus asked.

"I can't tell you that. It's a secret. Only Ledesmas know where it is." She sipped once more on her tea, put the cup down, and walked to the door.

"It's down in the cliff where the Roman hall is, isn't it?" Holly asked.

Professor LePawnee looked slightly irritated. She ignored the question and opened the door. "Inform me immediately if you find any clues that will allow us to find the spy. And please keep the missing paintings a secret."

Holly nodded and trudged out the door, disappointed that she hadn't received a reply.

"How do you know that the Flower of Creativity is in the cliff?" Brian asked once they'd left the office.

"I don't," said Holly. "But there were a bunch of butterflies fluttering around the sphinx in the Roman hall," said Holly. "Normal butterflies don't live indoors. And they can stay a while in the dark, but most of the time they would be outside in the sunlight. They're not moths."

"So you think those were Ledesma butterflies?" Brian asked.

Holly nodded. "But now we have something more important to worry about. There's a spy among us."

Detention

Once you have found the magic, you never want to go back.

In the next few months, Cuspidor was never far from Holly's mind. But since she was struggling to keep up in her classes, she couldn't focus as much as she wanted to on finding Cuspidor or his accomplice.

After having discussed it many times with her friends, they had come to the conclusion that only Professor Farouche could be the spy, despite LePawnee's trust in him. Every time Holly sat in his class, she tried to find some clue to prove that he was working for Cuspidor. But she never found anything, so she spent every free moment studying. She didn't want to repeat her failure at Donkleywood School here at Cliffony.

In late April, Villa Nonesuch's first leaves announced the arrival of spring. Holly didn't really notice, though. She was too busy practicing Creation and Deletion brushstrokes. An announcement was made that final exams were to take place the last week of May, and Holly wanted to be ready.

Even though she had improved on most brushstrokes, her attempts during Creation and Deletion still caused problems. Meanwhile, the Cannon Brushstroke in Professor Gobeli's class had become second nature, and ridding herself of the unfinished ermine was a piece of cake.

It was a Monday morning when Holly stumbled out of Villa Nonesuch—she was late again. Brian, Rufus, and Amanda were already sitting on Whitespot's back.

"Good luck at the pre-selection," said Cookie, petting Whitespot's head.

"Pre-selection?" Holly asked.

"The competitors for the Quadrennial Art Competition will be selected today," Rufus said. "Professor LePawnee announced that at the beginning of the school year."

Holly threw her hands over her mouth. "How was I supposed to know that it's today?"

"It is on the bulletin board," said Rufus. "I guess you did not read it."

Holly had never paid attention to the bulletin board. She remembered that LePawnee had mentioned the competition a few times, and Ileana had told her about it too, but for her it was never a pressing issue.

"You'd better get going," Cookie said.

"Wait," Holly cried, and ran back into Villa Nonesuch. She placed Tenshi in her backpack, came back out, and hopped on Whitespot's back.

Whitespot spread his wings and a minute later, they were flying high above the Griffin Hatchery. Holly was trembling inside. She was thinking about the Quadrennial Art Competition and that she should have studied for it. But she didn't even know what she would be tested on.

Whitespot reached Cliffony in record time. Far below, students were lining up at the entrance gate. As they landed, Mr. Hickenbottom sped down the stairs, as usual, shouting at them to clear the no-stopping zone. Holly sent Whitespot off to Market Square and lined up at the gate. Mr. Hickenbottom handed out the applications for the competition and flitted back up the stairs.

Ileana was already waiting in line. "I heard the competition will be very difficult this year," she said. "They want to limit it to seven contestants."

"Why is that?" Rufus asked.

"Seven is a lucky number," said Ileana. "And the professors don't want the competition to drag on for days."

"What do we have to do?" Holly asked.

"For the pre-selection, nothing really," said Ileana. "Gullveig will look deep inside you and see if you are good enough or not."

Holly was relieved. This was her way out: Gullveig would dismiss her before she even had to compete, so no one would ever find out that she hadn't prepared anything. But still, she was a bit worried that the oracle would look deep inside her and see that she was not talented enough to be a Gindar after all.

The line of students moved forward, and the crowd

pushed Holly up the stairs, along the entrance hall, and into the Grand Hall. The gong echoed loudly, the doors swung shut, and Professor LePawnee silenced the crowd with the gentle gesture of her hand.

"Welcome to the pre-selection for the Quadrennial Art Competition," said LePawnee as she stood up from the table. "Oracle Gullveig has carefully evaluated the competitors and will announce the selected students. This year, we will have seven contestants. Oracle Gullveig has taken many different aspects into consideration: talent, stamina, passion for art, eagerness to learn, and improvements you have made throughout the year. But, most of all, your potential was taken into account."

Holly relaxed. It seemed that she did not even have to talk to Gullveig. With the lack of talent that she had shown over the months in Creation and Deletion class, she was very unlikely to be selected.

Professor Bundo energetically swung himself up from his seat and pulled the curtain open. Amanda smiled.

"This year, we have decided to limit not only the number of applicants but the requirements as well," said Bundo. "Students under the age of eleven are not eligible—nor are former Unfinished."

Ileana looked disappointed.

"At this time, they are too fragile, and we don't want to risk anything happening to them," Bundo added.

"Get rid of them," yelled someone from the crowd. "They are scum."

A dozen other voices joined in, shouting nasty remarks. Holly noticed Gina and Lismahoon sitting among the crowd

of shouting students.

"Ignore them," said Holly, putting her arm around Ileana.

"Quiet," Professor LePawnee shouted sharply. The crowd immediately silenced. With a stern look, she admonished the crowd. "You should be ashamed of yourselves. The Unfinished have suffered for a long time. They don't deserve further humiliation." She sat down.

"I cannot believe they have this ridiculous age limit and did not mention it," said Rufus. "I was so ready for this competition." Unlike the others, Rufus was a few months short of being eleven.

The gong echoed, and Gullveig's voice roared out of the shell. "I have selected the following contestants: Serafina Abby—"

Serafina bolted forward eagerly and took her seat in the first row.

The gong sounded after each contestant's name.

"Eric Lismahoon."

Lismahoon shook Gina's hand and marched forward, his protruding lower jaw hanging down like always. It looked as if he were ready to catch a fly.

"I can't believe that lizard made it," Amanda said.

The gong echoed again. "Brian Findley."

"Wow," said Brian. "I can't believe this."

He went to the platform, shook Professor LePawnee's hand, and sat down in the first row.

Holly clapped harder than ever, but deep inside she was worried about what would happen. She had mixed feelings. On the one hand, she was hoping she would not have to compete because she hadn't studied, but on the other hand if she was not selected, all the students would know that she was a fake.

The gong was beating at a faster pace. Gullveig continued announcing the remaining contestants: Billy Dinroad and Calvin Kennicott.

"He did it again," Ileana said, looking jealously at her brother.

"And Holly O'Flanigan," Gullveig added.

Holly froze as the crowd around her applauded. Gullveig had actually called her name. She felt dizzy. Now she had to compete, and she knew she did not have the talent to meet everybody's expectations.

"Well done," said Amanda, putting her arm around Holly.

"I didn't do anything," Holly said as Amanda pushed her forward to Professor LePawnee.

The professor shook Holly's hand and congratulated her. Then she sat down next to Brian.

The gong sounded again.

"Gina Chillingham."

"Not that snake," Amanda's voice reverberated through the Grand Hall.

Gina walked to the front row, ignored the professor's outstretched hand, and pushed Lismahoon to the side. She sat down like a queen seizing her throne.

Professor LePawnee silenced the applauding students. "The seven contestants will be exempt from final exams."

Holly jumped up from the bench and cheered. At least there was something positive about all this.

The other six contestants joined her, shouting and jumping

up and down. No more worrying about the exams. Smiling, Holly flung her arms behind her head and leaned back.

"I guess we have a few weeks to get ready for the competition," Brian said.

Holly's excitement took a deep plunge. For a second, she had forgotten that she would have to compete in the contest instead of taking exams. Holly scowled as the applause around her ceased and the Grand Hall emptied. Now she would really embarrass herself in front of the whole academy.

"Study everything you can," Professor LePawnee told the competitors before leaving the Grand Hall.

That was easier said than done. There were millions of brushstrokes Holly didn't know. She could study for the next two hundred years and only memorize a fraction of them. She threw her backpack over her shoulder as the students squeezed their way out of the Grand Hall. Holly had lost her friends in the crowd and so she left alone. As she came out of the hall, Farouche pulled her to the side.

"So how did you fool Gullveig?" he asked.

"I didn't," Holly said.

"She didn't fool anybody." Brian had appeared from the crowd and stood by her side.

"Quiet," barked Farouche. "You both listen to me now. I don't like you sneaking into forbidden places."

Holly understood. Farouche wasn't angry about the pre-selection, but about them sneaking into Ravenscraig Lane.

"You think rules don't apply to you, don't you?" Farouche asked. "This way—now." He pushed Holly and Brian toward a spiral staircase that led into the cellar.

"Where are you going?" Rufus shouted from behind. He came running from the crowd of students.

"Perfect timing, Mr. Letterhead," said Farouche. "I think you might want to join your friends for detention."

"Why detention?" Rufus asked.

"For sneaking into Ravenscraig Lane." Professor Farouche grinned at Rufus.

"But that was months ago," Rufus protested.

"It's never too late for detention," said Professor Farouche, pushing the three down the staircase until they reached a dark cellar corridor. Lapia was standing in an alcove halfway along the corridor with her hand underneath her towering wig.

"Professor Lapia!" Holly yelled, trying to get her attention. Maybe she could help.

Swiftly, the professor pulled out her hand from underneath her wig and shot out from the niche. "Mortimor, what are you doing with these children?"

"Detention," Farouche said gruffly.

"You are not giving them detention without Leguthiandra's approval, are you?" Lapia asked.

Holly sighed with relief. Her plan to involve Professor Lapia in this matter was working.

Farouche held his breath. His head seemed to swell like a balloon about to explode. "I don't need authorization. As an instructor, I have the power to discipline students."

"I will not discuss this with you," replied Lapia. "Put the children in your office and come with me. Leguthiandra has cleared them of any wrongdoing."

Holly wondered why Lapia didn't want to take them directly

to LePawnee's office, but at least the headmistress would be informed about what Farouche was doing.

"I'll see you in Leguthiandra's office," Lapia said as she walked down the hallway. "And if anything happens to the children, I will hold you responsible."

Grudgingly, Farouche unlocked his office and pushed the kids inside.

The Flower of Creativity

You know that you have to leave magic behind because if you didn't, fantasy would become the only thing in your life.

Holly, Brian, and Rufus entered the office. It was filled from top to bottom with bookshelves. A grandfather clock stood against one of the walls. Dusty cobwebs revealed that Farouche's office hadn't been cleaned in years. In the middle of the room was a round mahogany table with four chairs.

"Sit down," said Farouche. "I'll get you some work to do while I'm gone." He left the room.

Holly sank into one of the chairs, listening to the antique grandfather clock strike six. But there was another sound as well.

Holly got back up, went to the clock, and put her ear

against the wall. The sound was coming from behind the clock. Holly jumped back as Farouche stumbled into the room with a towering stack of parchment.

He dropped his burden on the mahogany table. "Copy them," he said, pulling out a stack of blank parchment from one of the lower shelves. He planted an inkpot with three quills firmly on the table. "I'll be back shortly."

With a decisive click, the dungeon door fell shut. The sound reminded Holly of her lonely days in the attic of the Smoralls' mansion. But it was still better to get detention than being stuck with the Smoralls.

"Holy smokes. Look at that pile," Brian sighed. "That'll take us the whole weekend to copy."

"Professor LePawnee is going to get us out of this," Rufus said.

"Quiet," said Holly. "I hear something. I think it's..." She scooted back to the grandfather clock and put her ear against the wall. She flipped the case open and stopped the pendulum. Holly heard a voice far away.

"I think it's Cuspidor. I can hear something," said Holly. "What about you?"

"I don't hear a thing," Brian said.

Holly tapped on the wall. There was a hollow space behind it. She tried to move the clock, but it didn't budge.

Brian examined the inside of the clock case while Holly checked the outside. Accidentally, she pushed one of the gilded miniature columns next to the clock's face. There was a jolt, and the clock shifted to the side, giving way to a secret tunnel.

"Jeepers," said Holly. "I guess Farouche really does have

something to hide. Let's see where it leads."

"What if Farouche comes back," asked Rufus, fidgeting, "and sees we have not copied any of the parchment?"

Tenshi grunted and peeked out of Holly's backpack. He was holding the red twin feather that Holly had found in the mysterious box in Donkleywood. He pointed it at the stack of parchment and hopped out of the backpack.

"Wait a minute," said Rufus. "I have read about that feather."

He opened his backpack, took out a small book, and handed it to Holly.

"'Magical Objects Approved by the High Council,'" read Holly. She flipped through its pages.

"'Feather—the magic feather,'" she read aloud, as she reached the letter F. An illustration similar to the one in Tenshi's paw was painted next to the text. "'The magic feather is one of the few magical objects with a mind. In connection with the correct brushstroke, it can write essays, scientific research papers, and resolve mathematical problems on its own.'"

"Holy smokes," said Brian, grinning. "With that feather I wouldn't have to study anymore."

"And stay dumb for the rest of your life," Rufus added indignantly.

On one of the pages, Holly found the brushstroke that would activate the magic feather. She pulled out her paintbrush and followed the instructions.

A thread of ash-gray paint shot from her brush, encircling the feather, which propped itself up and began to write on the parchment. It flew over the pages. Each time a sheet was finished, the feather flicked another paper under its ink-filled tip and continued copying.

"Well, that problem is solved," said Holly, surprised for a moment that it worked out that well.

All of a sudden, Tenshi began to squeak. He pulled a book from one of the lower shelves and handed it to Holly.

"*Nukimais and their characteristics*," read Holly on the cover. "We don't have time for this now, Tenshi. I can learn about your species some other time."

Tenshi's head drooped and he sat on the floor.

"Let's go now," Brian said as he headed down the secret passage.

"We'll be back in a few minutes," Holly said to Tenshi.

Holly and Rufus swung their brushes and the tips illuminated the tunnel. The light stirred a few bats, which began to flutter around their heads.

"Amanda would hate that," Brian said.

"But Professor Gobeli would love it," Holly added. They shared a quick laugh.

The passage wound downward and ended at a door decorated with a painting of an orchid. Holly pushed the heavy door open. A dim light filtered into the tunnel from a circular hole in the center of a dome-like ceiling, revealing a gigantic cavern. A luminescent red flower, as big as a house, grew in the center.

Thousands of butterflies danced in the sunlight that shone on the blossom of the giant flower from the dome above. Like a waterfall gushing down a mountain, the butterflies dipped down into the blossom, then shot back up to the opening, and

disappeared into the sky. A constant flow of new butterflies kept the beam of sunlight in constant motion.

"It looks like a gigantic *Vanda coerulea*," Rufus said, his lower jaw dropping.

"*Vanda* what?" Brian asked.

"*Vanda coerulea*," repeated Rufus. "It is a rare species of orchid. They are from Asia. Usually they are blue, and they certainly do not grow in caverns. And they are never that big," he said. "Since it cannot be a *Vanda coerulea*, it must be something else."

"So what could it be?" Brian asked.

"Think, Brian," replied Holly. "Where do Ledesma butterflies go?"

Brian's eyes widened as if they were about to pop out of his head. "The Flower of Creativity."

A screech from Tenshi echoed down from Farouche's office. Holly spun around.

"Farouche must be on his way back," said Brian, dashing out of the cavern and into the tunnel.

"Rufus, run," said Holly, grabbing his hand.

Holly bolted after Brian, pulling Rufus behind her. As they reached the office, Holly shoved the grandfather clock back into place.

"We made it!" Holly said, totally out of breath.

The feather finished the last parchment just as Farouche turned the key in the dungeon door. Brian dropped the feather in his pocket as Holly grabbed the stack of parchment. The door opened, and Farouche entered.

"Here," said Holly briskly, dropping the pile of parchment

into Farouche's arms. "Can we go now?"

Farouche stared at the stack of parchment, nodded, and stepped aside.

The Quadrennial Art Competition

Always be careful not to lose touch with reality.

A few weeks before the Quadrennial Art Competition, Holly and Brian were in the library researching brushstrokes from previous competitions. The other students had already taken their final exams and were getting ready for summer break that started after the competition. Except for a few dwarfs cleaning the school grounds, Cliffony was empty.

"Fifty years ago, they had to create a swarm of green-dotted ladybugs," said Brian, flipping through an ancient book. "How stupid is that?"

Holly grimaced, pointing over Brian's shoulder at a passage. "And this is even more stupid. Here it says they once had to create a tower of cotton candy."

"Here's the task from the last contest," said Brian, pushing his glasses up onto the bridge of his nose. "It's a mathematical equation. What does that have to do with painting? I don't see a pattern here."

Holly was shocked. It seemed that even academics were important for the contest. How were they supposed to know these things? Nobody was teaching math at Cliffony.

"There's no pattern," Holly said, discouraged. "I guess we just have to wait and see what tasks we get." She opened one of the library windows and watched Mr. Hickenbottom chase some kids who were shooting firecrackers across the stairs. "I wish we had never been selected," she grumbled. "It'll be the worst day of my life."

Sooner than she liked, the big day arrived and the courtyard was prepared for the Quadrennial Art Competition. Flags displaying Cliffony's coat of arms fluttered on towering poles. Stands for the spectators had been set up along the school walls, and purple banners decorated the seating rows. A separate box overlooking the courtyard had been built for the professors. The seven competitors, dressed in velvet cloaks, were waiting in a room on the ground floor of the Tower of Bats.

"This competition is going to be a piece of cake," Calvin said. Holly watched as Ileana's brother made himself comfortable in a leather armchair. "Competing against first-year students is ridiculous." He looked indignantly at the other six contestants.

"What a show off," said Brian. "He thinks he's all that and a bag of marzipan griffins."

Holly peeked onto the courtyard through the only window

in the room. There was lots of hustle and bustle. The students and their parents were seated in the front rows. Holly thought of Grandpa Nikolas and, for a moment, she daydreamed that he would be sitting there, cheering her on. The back rows were filled with Ledesmas, dwarfs, and many creatures Holly had never even seen before.

The sound of trumpets on the battlements silenced the crowd. The professors paraded down the staircases to a triumphant fanfare. Professor LePawnee led a group of professors down the left staircase, while Farouche headed a second group on the right. In the center of the courtyard, the two lines met and headed for their seats. As the fanfare came to its finale, the professors sat down simultaneously, except for LePawnee. She remained standing.

"Magorians," the professor said. "Welcome to the Quadrennial Art Competition. Let's meet the competitors."

The trumpets blared again, and a dwarf opened the door to the waiting room.

"Line up behind me," the dwarf ordered.

Calvin raced forward, spearheading the group. Gina, Lismahoon, Serafina, and Billy Dinroad followed.

Holly trotted after them, toward the courtyard. Cheers welcomed the contestants. Holly could smell the freshly mowed grass as she marched toward the center. She kept her eyes fixed on the manicured lawn, trying to calm herself. What if she failed every single test? She knew she had some artistic strength, but her weaknesses were outnumbering them so far. Holly started trembling slightly. What if she embarrassed herself in front of the whole school?

"Look, there are the others," said Brian, waving at the first row where Rufus, Ileana, Amanda, and Cookie were seated.

"Three tasks will be given to the contestants," announced Professor LePawnee as they reached the center. "The judges will grade the tasks. Each round, a maximum of twelve points will be awarded and contestants with the lowest points will be disqualified. The totals from the first two rounds will be added to determine the two finalists. Let us begin."

The trumpets sounded from the battlements again. Bundo stood up, marched down the stairs toward the contestants, and asked them to form a circle.

He pulled out his paintbrush and drew a circle and three triangles in the air.

A thread of red paint shot out of his brush and turned into a hovering fireball.

"I have the honor of announcing the first task," said Bundo. "Each of the contestants must create a vase."

"Why am I not surprised?" Holly whispered to Brian. "A creation brushstroke, of course."

The professor silenced the crowd. "There is more to this task. The contestants will have to create a vase that withstands heat." He pointed at the ten-foot wide fireball hovering in the air. "The vase that lasts the longest in the fire will win." Bundo pulled a velvet pouch from his pocket. "Each of the contestants will pick a disc with a number on it so we can determine the order."

Holly picked a disc and flipped it over. Number seven. She was last. Holly's head drooped. Going last was what she had dreaded. The expectations of the judges would be even higher

after everybody else had demonstrated their skills.

Bundo swung his brush. Bright yellow paint shot at the fireball, which began to spin, sending off waves of heat.

Holly smoothed her hair back and wiped the sweat off her forehead.

Being first, Eric Lismahoon stepped forward. He raised his brush, and a thin thread of ash-gray paint entered the fireball. Within a split second, a silver vase hovered in the center of the blazing fire. The vase lasted about five seconds before it liquefied and the paint shot back into the brush as if nothing had happened.

Holly grinned. She knew she was being petty, but she was glad that Lismahoon's creation was so short-lived, since he was a friend of Gina's.

Brian went next. A stream of metallic paint came out of his brush and a vase of pure gold formed. It was not a great piece of artwork, but it was gold. While Holly counted the seconds, she wondered how Brian had created something in color. He must have studied color painting on his own. Holly waited for the vase to dissolve. After a short time, she stopped counting. "Yes, he did it," she said as the vase slowly liquefied. Brian had done better than Lismahoon.

"You guys should know that copper is much stronger than gold and silver," said Calvin, grinning. "It liquefies at around 1080 Celsius." Calvin swung his brush and a copper vase appeared. It lasted a full minute in the fire.

Holly gulped. She didn't know what she would do, but at least Calvin was better than Lismahoon, and hopefully better than Gina as well.

Nervously, Serafina pulled on her pigtails as her tin vase liquefied within seconds. The same disaster happened to Billy Dinroad who had opted for brass.

Holly's mind was running through the whole spectrum of possible materials. Plastic, wood, paper, leather. She knew that all this would go up in flames immediately. But what about iron? It was harder than anything else. Holly tried to remember the brushstroke for it, but couldn't.

"Brian, what is the brushstroke for iron?" she asked.

Brian shook his head. He didn't know either.

"I know it's something with a rectangle," Holly said.

Gina stepped closer to the fireball, grinning at Holly. "Thank you," she said, painting a rectangle with a line underneath in the air. Ivory-black paint shot from her brush into the fire and created an iron vase.

"She stole my idea!" Holly yelled.

Nobody heard her amidst the applause that erupted from the crowd.

"You're next, Gindar," said Gina with a malicious smile on her face.

Villa Littlemore

Reality is as important as fantasy. As much as fantasy allows you to dream, reality grounds you.

As slowly as a snail, Holly trudged to the fireball, hoping she would come up with a solution at the last minute. Platinum, titanium, quartz, shot through her mind. But she didn't know the brushstrokes for them. Panicked, she glanced at Rufus. Tenshi was hopping up and down in Rufus' lap, waving at her with his fluffy paws. He was so cute compared to the flowerpot-Nukimai she had created in the exam.

"A flowerpot-Nukimai," Holly whispered to herself. "That's it. I have to create a clay flowerpot. It's kind of a vase."

Something made out of clay would harden in the fire and not dissolve. After months of learning the brushstroke for flowerpots, Holly was confident that she would be able to create one now.

Relieved, she swung her brush. A few threads of paint shot into the fireball and a flowerpot formed in the fire.

Holly jumped and cheered, "I did it!"

She stared at her creation. The flowerpot was crooked, but that didn't matter. It was the material that counted. And that material was clay.

The crowd and the judges whispered. Holly knew they were talking about her choice. It was not a vase, though the flowerpot was in the same family. She wondered if that would fail her, but as she counted the seconds, the flowerpot lasted longer than anybody else's creation. After about two minutes, applause erupted and increased with every second the soft clay hardened in the fire.

Finally, Professor Bundo stepped forward sucked the fireball back into his brush. The flowerpot dropped to the ground and broke. Bundo walked back to the other professors. They argued among themselves for a while until Professor LePawnee stood up and raised her hand.

"We have carefully evaluated the results of the first task. Four contestants will enter the next round. Professor Kaplin, would you be so kind and give us the results of the judges?"

Kaplin pulled his reading glasses down on his nose and unrolled a piece of parchment. "Three points for Serafina Abbey, who gave her best when creating a tin vase. Five points for Billy Dinroad for creating a brass vase that lasted a bit longer. Brian Findley receives seven points for the use of gold. Eric Lismahoon used silver and, therefore, gets eight points. Calvin Kennicott receives ten points for his astuteness in using copper. And Gina Chillingham receives the highest number, twelve points, for using iron. However, the goal was to create a vase that lasts in the fire. Nevertheless, Gina's vase dissolved at 1536°C. Therefore, we had to subtract one point. So her final tally is eleven points."

The crowd applauded, as Gina waved like a queen to the spectators.

"Then there is Holly O'Flanigan," Professor Kaplin began, and the crowd silenced immediately. "We have discussed how many points she should be awarded. She created a flowerpot and not a vase, as requested. However, she has shown cleverness and wit by using a soft material that hardens, rather than a hard material that melts. Because of some disagreement among the judges—" Kaplin paused and glared angrily at Farouche, "Holly O'Flanigan receives eleven points."

"Shoot" Gina's voice echoed through the courtyard.

The crowd erupted in applause again.

"I passed," cried Holly. "I can't believe it."

She danced around for a moment until she saw Brian's sad face. She had completely forgotten that he had just lost. Holly stopped and went over to him.

"I'm sorry," she said. "It was only because you had to be one of the first ones."

"That's okay," said Brian. "Just make sure Gina doesn't win."

Brian trudged with Serafina and Billy to the first row in the audience.

"Second round," Professor LePawnee said.

Professor Gobeli stood up. "Contestants please move out

of the center of the courtyard."

They walked to the Tower of Bats. The trumpets blared again, and Professor Gobeli pointed her brush into the air. She made a series of brushstrokes. Paint in different greens whirled high into the sky. It thickened and turned into a tornado that swooped down to the courtyard. The walls of Cliffony shook as the tornado hit the lawn, split the ground open, and vanished into the gorge it had just created.

An eerie silence hung over the courtyard. Then a rumbling sound echoed as if an earthquake had hit Cliffony. The courtyard shook, and a massive birch tree was pushed up from below. The earth around the bottom of the trunk closed up and the lawn began to grow. It only took a moment until it looked as if this tree had always been standing in the courtyard.

"Cool!" Lismahoon said. "A tree!"

"It's so not a tree, you idiot," Gina said, nudging him. "It's a tree house."

The giant tree house was twice the size of Villa Nonesuch. Its massive branches reached into the sky, towering over the courtyard like one of the castle turrets.

"I would like to welcome Villa Littlemore," Professor Gobeli announced.

"Thank you for having me," said Villa Littlemore in a deep, male voice, which echoed through the courtyard.

"Students, the fireball task showed your ability to create things," said Gobeli. "This task will show your problem-solving skills. Each contestant gets five minutes to count all of Villa Littlemore's leaves. Only two contestants will reach the final round. We will start in the same order as previously set. Mr.

Lismahoon, would you begin please?"

Lismahoon nervously chewed on his upper lip. Obviously, he didn't know what to do. Holly didn't know either. If she climbed Villa Littlemore and started counting the leaves, she would be sitting up there for the next two hundred years. If she used the magic brush, she would have to know which brushstroke to use. And she couldn't think of a brushstroke that counted leaves.

"Time is running—now." Gobeli started the stopwatch in her hand.

Lismahoon climbed up the tree house and began counting the leaves.

"Time is up," the professor said after five minutes had elapsed.

Lismahoon climbed down, with his pants torn and blood oozing from a scratch on his elbow. He scowled as Gobeli asked him for his estimate.

"I have no idea," muttered Lismahoon. "Maybe twenty-thousand leaves?"

Professor Kaplin wrote down the number. Calvin was next.

He strutted to Villa Littlemore, holding his brush tightly in his hand.

"Time is running—now," Gobeli said again.

Calvin used his brush. A thread of white paint curled around his feet and lifted him up to the treetop. He counted the leaves of one branch, took a piece of parchment out of his pocket, and started writing. When the time had elapsed, he landed safely on the lawn.

"What is your guess?" Gobeli asked.

"According to my calculations, there are about one-hundred-fifty-seven-thousand leaves," said Calvin. "You just have to use mathematical projection to estimate the total number."

Holly glanced over to Gina, wondering how she would count the leaves.

Gina scoffed. "Give up, O'Flanigan. You have already lost," she said as she strode confidently over to Villa Littlemore.

Holly was curious to see what Gina was going to do. But at the same time she was worried about how she would count the leaves herself.

"Time is running—now," Gobeli shouted across the courtyard again.

Gina dropped down flat on the lawn and mumbled something into the grass. Then she jumped up, made a brushstroke, and created a floating mountain of sugar. Thousands of ants crawled out of the ground, sped up Villa Littlemore's trunk, and covered every leaf.

Villa Littlemore giggled until Gobeli shouted, "Time is up."

Gina lifted her brush, and the ants darted down the tree. They gathered underneath the hovering sugar-mountain.

"How many leaves are there?" Gobeli asked.

"They will tell you," said Gina, pointing at the black mass of ants that crawled across the lawn.

The black mass of ants started to form numbers. It reminded Holly of what she had seen in sports events when masses of people create patterns that could be seen from a bird's-eye perspective.

The ants crawled around and slowly came to a halt. They had created the number 158,700. Gina grinned, satisfied. The ants moved again. The sign "~" appeared in front of the number.

"Approximately?" Gina shrieked. "Stupid ants. Can't you be more exact?"

Clenching the brush in her hand, she made a brushstroke and dropped the sugar-mountain to the ground. Within seconds, the ants loaded up the sugar and disappeared into the lawn.

The sound of applause and stomping filled the courtyard, showing that the audience had enjoyed Gina's show.

"I didn't know we could ask someone to do the work for us." Holly was surprised, but did not have the time to think about it.

"Holly O'Flanigan. Next!" Professor Gobeli announced.

Cuspidor's Accomplice

Reality needs fantasy to escape everyday boredom. Fantasy needs reality to build a foundation on which to thrive.

Holly trembled. Sweat was running down her forehead and dripping from her nose. She had no idea what to do now. Could she find someone who would help her count the leaves?

She trudged to Villa Littlemore, hoping for a miracle to happen.

"Time is running—now," Professor Gobeli hollered.

The only one who could help her now would be the tree house himself. What if she just asked him? It couldn't hurt to ask.

Holly knocked on the massive trunk. "Excuse me."

"Yes," a voice sounded while the leaves shook.

"I'm Holly O'Flanigan. I have the pleasure of living in a tree house. Villa Nonesuch is a good friend of mine."

"What a coincidence," boomed the tree house. "She is my cousin. She's a sweetheart, isn't she?"

"Yes, she is. But I'm here because I have a problem. I have to pass this test, and I was wondering if you could just tell me how many leaves you have," Holly said politely and added a "please."

"I don't know if I'm allowed to tell you," said Villa Littlemore. "But on the other hand, nobody has told me not to give out this information. Since you have asked so politely, I don't see why I shouldn't help you."

Holly stroked the bark of the giant trunk.

"The exact number is 158,707," said the tree house, purring like a tiger.

"Thank you so much," said Holly. She ran across the courtyard to the professors and told them the total number.

Professor Gobeli swung her brush and with a rumble, Villa Littlemore sank back into the ground, waving his branches goodbye to Holly.

The professors whispered among themselves until Professor Kaplin stood up.

"We judges have decided that Eric Lismahoon receives one point for trying. Calvin Kennicott showed his mathematical talent by using projections. He came close to the actual number. He receives nine points. Gina Chillingham not only put up a dramatic show, but also showed that she has the means to resolve problems by commanding ants to do what she wants. However, the number was off by a few leaves. Therefore Gina

receives eleven points," Gobeli said.

"I'm so good," said Gina, grinning.

Holly squeezed her eyes shut, waiting for her points.

"Holly O'Flanigan has resorted to something nobody had expected," said Professor Gobeli. "She asked for help. As simple as this solution might be, it is a completely legitimate approach—even though some might think it's not." Gobeli glanced over at Farouche. "The number of leaves was correct, and Holly O'Flanigan will be awarded eleven points."

Professor LePawnee stood up. "The total points for the first two rounds are as follows: Eric Lismahoon nine points, Calvin Kennicott nineteen points, Gina Chillingham twenty-two points, and Holly O'Flanigan twenty-two points. We have a tie."

"I can't believe that two first-years eliminated me!" Calvin bellowed, leaving the courtyard.

Brian came running toward Holly and hugged her.

"You did it," he said. "Asking the tree house to give you the number of leaves was brilliant."

Holly smiled. She had beaten all the other competitors except Gina. Even if she lost now, she would still get second place. There was nothing to be embarrassed about anymore. For a moment, all her self-doubt was gone, and Holly was happier than ever.

"Gina Chillingham and Holly O'Flanigan are our final contestants," announced Professor LePawnee. "The final task is the most difficult in the history of the Quadrennial Art Competition. There is danger involved."

Holly's heart began to beat fast. What kind of danger was

she talking about? Was her life at risk?

"I will stay close to the contestants," said LePawnee. "Just to make sure they are safe."

LePawnee stood up and glided down the stairs and across the courtyard to Holly and Gina.

"For this task, absolute darkness is required," said the professor. "The contestants will be fighting against an Unfinished."

"Cool," Holly whispered to Brian. "I can handle that."

She had freed herself a dozen times from the rabbit and the ermine. It shouldn't be a problem to rid herself of another Unfinished.

"I guess Professor Farouche did you a favor after all," Brian said and went back to his seat.

All the professors stood up, solemnly marched to the beat of drums down to the courtyard, and formed a circle around Holly and Gina.

"Professor Gobeli, would you please darken the courtyard?" LePawnee said. "At times, you in the audience might not see much of the event. I apologize, but darkness is absolutely imperative. Otherwise, the Unfinished will fade and die."

Gobeli clapped twice, and a black tornado approached the courtyard. As it drew nearer, Holly noticed that it wasn't a tornado but a swarm of giant bats—thousands of them. Gobeli clapped once more. The bats fluttered to the battlements, spread their wings, and like a camera shutter closing a lens, they formed a blackout dome. Darkness engulfed the courtyard. Only the flickering light of a few torches remained.

Murmurs rumbled throughout the crowd. "We shall start

now." LePawnee silenced them. "The winner of this round will win the entire competition."

Holly could barely see the judges standing in a circle around her, but she heard them breathing, as much as she heard her heart pulsating rapidly.

"I have a surprise for you," Holly heard Farouche's voice in the darkness.

Two people approached. It was Farouche holding a chain that was attached to the neck of a boy. Holly didn't see the boy clearly until he was but a few feet away. She gasped when she realized it was the Unfinished she had seen in the ward. His body still consisted of pencil lines, and his eyes sparkled in the darkness.

"It is an unfinished human," Gina hissed.

Holly's confidence vanished in an instance. She could handle an unfinished rabbit without a problem, but a human?

Farouche handed the boy a paintbrush and released him from the chains. Instead of leaping forward and attacking as the rabbit had, the boy lifted his brush and made a brushstroke. White paint shot out of his brush and hit Holly on the chest. She staggered back. The paint bounced off and hit Gina, too. There, it bounced off again and returned to the Unfinished, creating a hovering triangle of white paint between them. Holly watched the thread of paint slowly turn blood red. The Unfinished was sucking her blood through the paint. Holly was now connected with both the boy and Gina, just as she had been with the unfinished rabbit in Farouche's class.

You are a very accomplished Gindar, said the boy with the same soothing tone the unfinished rabbit had spoken with. Holly knew immediately his voice was in her mind because his lips were not moving. She was about to say that she was not a Gindar at all when she remembered that the Unfinished only wanted to distract her.

She is not a Gindar, Gina's voice echoed in Holly's mind. *I'm the real Gindar.*

Gina, this is not the time to discuss this, said Holly, getting more worried as she noticed how the Unfinished kept sucking the blood out of both of them.

No, it is the time, cried Gina. *Ever since you came here, you have tried to take away what is rightfully mine.*

Gina, if you don't stop this now, the Unfinished is going to kill us, Holly said.

You're trying to distract us from the real issue here, Gina shouted furiously.

Holly lifted her brush. *I can't wait any longer, Gina. In a few minutes I won't be able to free myself.*

Gina, do you want to let her get away like that? the Unfinished asked calmly.

Gina clenched her fists, lifted her brush, and made a brushstroke. A blade formed on the tip and shot at Holly. She felt pain in her hand, dropped her brush, and tumbled to the ground.

You'll get what you deserve, Gina hissed. *Everybody who turned against me will suffer. Cuspidor will take over Magora.*

You are the one who helped Cuspidor, not Farouche, Holly said, flabbergasted. She could not believe it. Gina was the spy they had been looking for.

29

Chaos

Without a real foundation, fantasy will eventually disappear and leave you stranded to deal with everyday problems.

Holly crawled on all fours, searching for her brush. She was so angry that she did not feel the pain in her hand anymore.

Gina laughed and made a brushstroke. It took the Unfinished by surprise. The thread of white paint ripped in the middle, and Gina was free.

Holly felt weaker with every drop of blood that crept through the thread of white paint. Then she heard LePawnee scream. Panicked, she felt her way along the grass.

"Professor LePawnee? What happened? Are you all right?" Holly called.

Cries from the audience filled the courtyard. Hundreds of voices rose above the sound of footsteps. Holly kept searching the ground, hoping she would find her brush. Finally, she felt the smooth bristles. Relieved, she ran her fingers up to the handle. But there was something attached to the handle—it was a hand.

Holly felt her way up along the arm until she realized that it was LePawnee. Holly lifted the arm. It was lying limp in her hand. She felt the professor's pulse. She was still alive but seemed unconscious.

Too bad she had to get hurt, the Unfinished laughed.

Leave her alone, Holly shouted.

Determined, but trembling, she focused on the thread of paint. For the first time in her life, Holly was prepared to kill someone. She was angry that the Unfinished wanted to destroy Magora and take away the lives of people who cared about her. "You will not get my blood," she said.

She channeled all her energy and visualized how she could break the thread. And it worked.

No, you can't do that, the Unfinished whined as the blood flooded out of his body and back into Holly's.

Holly felt her strength coming back. Within minutes, she had gotten back most of her blood. She drew an X in the air with her brush. The thread of paint ripped in the middle, and the Unfinished tumbled back, screaming out loud.

Holly used the Cannon Brushstroke. A rock detached itself from the Tower of Bats, sped toward the dome, and knocked a few bats aside.

A beam of sunshine lightened up the courtyard and

unveiled a scene of disaster. The stands were empty, and the spectators roamed around aimlessly. All the Ledesmas were lying on the ground, unconscious.

"Professor LePawnee, please wake up," said Holly, fanning air into her expressionless face.

Every part of the professor's body was limp, yet her pulse was still beating. Holly peeked into the professor's lotus and jumped back to her feet. There was not a single butterfly in the bone lotus. Holly panicked. Hadn't the professor said that the Ledesmas would die if the butterflies left permanently? What was she supposed to do? She spotted Brian and sped across the entire length of the courtyard to him.

"Hurry," she shouted out of breath as she came to an abrupt halt. "The butterflies are gone. There must be something wrong with the Flower of Creativity. That's why all the Ledesmas are unconscious. We've got to get to the Flower of Creativity—now."

"I will go find Ileana," Rufus said. "We lost her in the chaos. I will catch up with you."

"All right," Holly said as Rufus took off.

Holly raced into the Tower of Bats. Brian and Amanda followed. They ran down the stairs and headed straight to Farouche's office. The dungeon door was wide open. Holly peered inside the office.

"Nobody here," she said, tiptoeing past the dusty bookshelves.

The grandfather clock had been moved aside, and the secret passage was already open.

"I bet Farouche is down there in the cave where the Flower

of Creativity is," said Holly. "It's his office after all."

"But LePawnee said that only Ledesmas know where the flower is," Amanda said. "Farouche is not a Ledesma."

"We'd better find out what's going on," said Holly. "If we don't get the butterflies back, Professor LePawnee and the other Ledesmas will die."

Holly darted down the tunnel until she reached the door with the orchid painting, which was also wide open. The Flower of Creativity still stood as grandly as before. But the butterflies that once had fluttered up and down the beam of sunlight had now disappeared.

"Where are the butterflies?" Brian asked.

Holly noticed a trail of a transparent liquid on the floor. It was leading from the flower to a door in the opposite wall. She got down on her knees and smelled it.

"I think I know where they are," Holly said as she dipped her finger in the syrup-like liquid.

"Where?" Brian asked.

"Someone has lured them away with a trail of nectar," said Holly, smelling the sweet liquid on her finger. She pointed at the opposite wall.

Brian jumped forward and peeked through a crack in the door. "It's the Roman Hall. I can see the marble statues," he said, swinging the door open.

The Roman Hall hadn't changed at all. The rubble was still piled up, the planks to the Gallery of Wonders still leaned against the frame of the door, and the giant hole still hadn't been repaired. Holly was about to step inside when the growl of a sphinx stopped her.

"I completely forgot about you," said Holly, remembering the second door in the hall that was protected by the sphinx. "Can we pass?"

"You are coming from the opposite side," said the sphinx. "I'm supposed to stop people from entering the cavern, not leaving. So if you want, you may leave."

Holly hopped over the pile of rubble and followed the red line to the hole in the wall.

"Look, the line leads directly down there," she said.

Brian swung his brush and illuminated the tunnel. "Let's go."

The light of the paintbrush startled hundreds of bats. Panicked, Amanda screeched, flailing her arms over her head.

"Quiet," Holly said. "I can hear something."

A voice echoed deep down in the hole. "Help. Please help me."

Holly raced down the tunnel, leaving Brian and Amanda behind. A dim light in the far distance illuminated the rocky path ahead of her. The tunnel took a turn and merged into a cavern the size of a sports arena.

Holly froze. She was standing amid hundreds of paintings. The entire cavern was stacked from top to bottom. Some paintings were the size of windows; others were as tiny as stamps. Some were painted on silk, some on canvas. Every kind of painting imaginable was piled up in the cavern. Wooden scaffolding led up to some of the stacks. In the center of the cavern hovered a giant glass sphere the size of a hot air balloon.

"We found them," Brian said as he entered. He pointed

at the glass sphere that was filled with thousands of Ledesma butterflies.

"Please help me," the voice echoed through the cavern again. It sounded panicked.

Holly followed the voice. She saw two figures in between stacks of paintings.

Holly swung her brush and illuminated the cavern.

"It's Farouche," Brian said.

"And Professor Lapia," Holly said, looking in bewilderment at the two instructors. "What are you doing?"

Farouche was lying on the ground, his hands tied behind his back, and Professor Lapia was gagging him with a scarf. His leg was bleeding. A smile flitted over Lapia's face when she saw Holly.

"Thank heavens," said Lapia. "He wanted to destroy the butterflies."

Instinctively, Holly pointed her brush at Farouche, then a voice sounded behind her.

"No!" yelled the voice.

Holly spun around. Rufus was standing in the cavern with Ileana by his side. "Not him," Rufus said. "Her!"

"What do you mean 'her'?" Holly asked.

"Farouche is not the spy—it is Professor Lapia," Rufus said. "She is lying."

Burma

Everyday problems can destroy a world of fantasy. It is best to deal with these problems first before entering such a realm. Once the problems are resolved, go back to fantasy and enjoy it because without it, reality could become dull and boring.

Holly turned back to the professors. Lapia laughed cunningly, pointing her brush at Holly.

"Drop your brush right now," Lapia said.

Holly lowered her brush and let go of the handle. She was totally confused. Never in her wildest dreams had she ever thought that Professor Lapia was the spy.

"Well done, Mr. Letterhead," said Lapia. "How did you find out?"

"The day we were in your office, I noticed a painting of

Burma on the wall," Rufus said. "It was a gate painting."

"I guess I didn't pull you away in time," Lapia said.

"I researched gate paintings and found there is only one Burma gate painting in Magora," said Rufus. "That painting was supposed to be in the Gallery of Wonders and not in your office. And then I came across a very surprising fact. I found out that the word 'lapia' means butterfly in Burmese."

"So that's why you got that book on Asian languages?" Brian said.

"Yes," said Rufus. "I could not make sense of all this. This is why I did not tell you anything. It was not until I saw the Ledesmas in the courtyard that it all made sense."

"What makes sense?" Amanda asked.

Holly's mouth dropped wide open. "Now I get it. Remember the first day we met Professor Lapia?"

"Yes, that was strange," said Amanda. "She stepped in griffin poo and said it tasted horrible."

Holly recalled what she had learned from her research paper in science class back in Donkleywood. "Butterflies have sensors on their feet and can taste with them," she said.

"Are you trying to say that Professor Lapia is a butterfly?" Brian asked.

"Not a butterfly," said Holly. "But something close to a butterfly—a Ledesma." Holly took a deep long look into the instructor's eyes. "You are one, aren't you? Only a Ledesma would know where the Flower of Creativity is."

Lapia laughed frantically and pulled off her wig. A thick scar stretched around her elongated bald head. "Yes, I was a Ledesma. My Ledesma name was Butterfly."

"Professor LePawnee told us about Butterfly on the day we came to Magora," Rufus said. "She told us that she traveled to Asia. When she came back, she didn't want to share her knowledge anymore."

"That was me," Lapia said.

Holly stared at the woman's scar. She did not believe it. It looked almost the same as the one Professor Farouche had.

"Is he a Ledesma, too?" Holly asked, pointing at Farouche.

Lapia nodded. "He had the same operation as I had, but he didn't do it voluntarily."

"What do you mean?" Holly asked.

"After I refused to share my knowledge, I was exiled to the land of Cuspidor by the High Council. They hoped that he would destroy me," said Lapia. "But instead, Cuspidor offered me a deal. He would give me an operation that would close my bone lotus and change my face. I could return to Magora without anybody knowing who I was. And I agreed. Farouche, on the other hand, was pressured by Cuspidor a long time ago to have this operation."

"What did Cuspidor want in return for your operation?" Ileana asked.

"He wanted two things. One of the two was the paintings in the Gallery of Wonders," Lapia said. "And so I told him about the hidden entrance. His seahorses drilled a hole, and his army carried the gallery to this cavern."

"And what was the other?" Holly asked.

"It was you," said Lapia. "Cuspidor wanted the new Gindar."

Holly hadn't been sure if the evil duke really was after her, but now that Lapia had said it out loud, Holly began to shake. He really did want to destroy her.

"You might have given Cuspidor the paintings, but Holly is still free," Brian said.

Lapia laughed hysterically. "This was all a plan, you dummy. When Farouche tried to give you detention, I was the one who told him to lock you in his office."

Holly remembered what had happened and how she had thought it didn't make sense at the time. She had wondered why Lapia didn't take them all to LePawnee's office. Now Holly knew that it was part of Lapia's plan.

"You said you were going to inform Professor LePawnee," Holly said.

"But instead, I informed Cuspidor that you were in Farouche's office," said Lapia. "I knew that Cuspidor would call you, and you would discover the Flower of Creativity."

"But why did you want me to find it?" Holly asked.

"I knew that if anything ever happened to the Ledesmas, you would go back to the Flower of Creativity where nobody would be around to notice your disappearance. Then I could catch you and bring you to Cuspidor."

"You could have caught her right here the first time," Brian said.

"I needed a good alibi in case something went wrong," Lapia said. "I suggested to LePawnee to use an Unfinished for the last task of the Quadrennial Art Competition. Once it was dark in the courtyard, I snuck out, lay the trail of nectar, and lured the butterflies into the glass sphere."

"You fooled us from the very first moment," Holly said. She felt anger rising in every inch of her body. If she'd had her brush, she would have shot a dozen blades toward Lapia. But it was lying at her feet, and Lapia was pointing her brush directly at Holly.

"I believe Professor Farouche ruined your plan," Rufus said.

"Yes," said Lapia. "Everything worked out until he showed up here a few moments ago."

At that precise moment, Farouche moved under Lapia's foot. She lost balance and fell forward on the ground.

Holly knew this was the moment to act. She reached down quickly and picked up her brush.

Lapia gained control again and aimed. Blades shot out. They raced toward Holly.

"Take cover!" Holly yelled to her friends as she made the Cannon Brushstroke.

She threw herself on the ground and watched as the boulder bounced off one of the walls and shot directly toward the glass sphere.

"Oh no," Holly cried. "It's not supposed to head in that direction. Everybody watch out!"

Brian, Rufus, and Ileana jumped behind a rock, but Amanda froze in place.

"Amanda, get down!" Holly yelled with her arms covering her head.

It was too late. The sphere with the butterflies shattered into pieces. A hailstorm of glass showered over them. Amanda dropped to the ground, bleeding. Lapia tried to hide behind some scaffolding, but the glass blasted through the air and covered her with splinters that sent her reeling back into a pile of paintings.

Holly jumped back up and sped to Amanda. Chips of glass covered her skin.

"It hurts," Amanda said, propping herself up.

Blood was dripping off her face.

"You're seriously injured," said Holly as Ileana and Rufus came over. "We'll have to take you back."

"Come and give me a hand," Brian shouted from the stack of paintings where Lapia was lying. "She's unconscious. We have to tie her up before she wakes up."

"Go ahead and help Brian," said Ileana. "I'll take care of Amanda."

Amanda swung her arm around Ileana and limped back up the tunnel with her.

Holly and Rufus went over to Brian and helped him restrain Lapia.

"I totally forgot about Farouche," Holly said. "You go and take Lapia back to Cliffony, and I will free the professor."

Brian and Rufus dragged Lapia by her arms. Thousands of butterflies danced and fluttered around them. Like a garland of multicolored flowers, the Ledesma butterflies followed the boys up the tunnel.

Holly ran to Professor Farouche, who was still lying on the same spot where Lapia had left him tied up. Holly picked up a piece of glass and cut the ropes.

Farouche jerked his head and slightly opened his eyes. Holly ungagged him.

"I'm so sorry I suspected you of being the spy," said Holly. "Are you all right?"

"My leg hurts, but I think I'm all right," Farouche said. "I do need your help to walk though."

"Put your arm around my shoulder," said Holly.

The professor slung his arm around Holly's neck and, with her help, he limped up the tunnel.

Once they had reached the Roman Hall, Farouche dropped onto the rubble, exhausted. Then he searched his whole body until he said, "I think my paintbrush must have fallen out of my pocket. Can you get it, please?"

"Sure," Holly said.

She ran back down the tunnel. When she reached the cavern, she noticed a soft blue light from above. Now that the glass sphere was gone, a giant dome was visible, spanning half the ceiling. It seemed to be made of blue-tinted crystal, and it separated the cavern from water above. The tip of the dome peeked out above the surface.

Holly recognized the crystal. These were the domes of the abandoned caverns she had seen in Lake Santima on the first day of their arrival.

Suddenly, a sizzling sound echoed behind her. Holly veered around. Three flying seahorses had blocked the tunnel.

Holly staggered backward farther into the cavern. What were Cuspidor's helpers doing here? A sudden fear overcame her. She was all alone.

Suddenly, Cuspidor's voice echoed through the cavern, louder than ever.

"Holly," he said.

"Stop entering my mind," yelled Holly, hammering her fists against her temples.

"I'm not in your mind—I'm right here," Cuspidor said.

A giant figure in a hooded black cloak stepped out from behind a towering stack of paintings. The shadow of the paintings covered the cloaked figure in darkness. Holly squinted. She couldn't see anything but the black cloak that seemed to hover in the air like a ghost.

The figure approached, yet continued to lurk within the gloomy shadows.

"Cuspidor," whispered Holly. Her heart was beating so hard it felt as if it could rip her chest open.

"That is what people call me," said the giant figure, "but my real name is S.A. Lokin."

Holly staggered backward toward the tunnel, but the seahorses resisted, pushing her farther into the center of the cavern.

"Finally we meet," Cuspidor said.

"What do you want from me?"

"I want you, Holly. I want the only Gindar left in Magora."

"Everybody's saying I'm a Gindar, but I'm not," said Holly. "I wish I were as talented as one."

Cuspidor laughed loudly. "You don't believe in yourself, do you? But it doesn't matter anymore because now you are mine."

Holly snorted, clenched her fists, and yelled, "I'm not yours. I don't belong to anybody. Who do you think you are? And why are you hiding your face?" She stomped her feet on

the ground like a raging bull, and tightly held her brush. "You want to get rid of me, don't you?"

Cuspidor laughed again and then whispered, "No, Holly. I need you. Without you, I could never take over Magora and become what I want."

"And what do you want to become?" Holly asked.

Cuspidor laughed. His cloaked hands reached for the hood and slowly pulled it back.

Holly could not believe what she saw.

Cuspidor's True Nature

For me, reality is as important as fantasy. Both are intertwined, and I could not live without either of them.

Holly stumbled back, and her brush dropped to the ground. With a thud, she landed on a rock.

"J-j-jeepers," stuttered Holly as Cuspidor's face became visible.

"I want to be completed," boomed Cuspidor. He ripped open his black cloak and threw it over his shoulders. "I don't want to be an Unfinished any longer."

Holly stared at the pencil lines that outlined Cuspidor's head. She had never seen an Unfinished with so few lines before. Those she had seen in the ward were recognizable as humans, but Cuspidor was nothing but a sketchy human outline. He had no facial features, only a few pencil lines, indicating where eyes, nose, and mouth were supposed to be. His body didn't look much different. Only his feet and calves had been completed. The rest of his body consisted of lines only.

Holly felt sick to her stomach. "Who left you like this?" she asked.

"Enough questions," Cuspidor boomed. "It's time for you to say goodbye. Soon your blood will run through my veins. It will make me the most powerful Gindar of all time."

Frantically, Holly searched behind her back for the brush she had dropped on the ground.

Cuspidor pulled out a long black brush from underneath his cloak. He drew a few lines in the air.

Before Holly could lift up her own brush, a thread of white paint hit her chest. She fell backward and watched as her blood crept through the white thread toward Cuspidor. The cavern around her became blurry. Just as she had heard the Unfinished rabbit in her mind while it was sucking her blood, she heard Cuspidor's voice now.

Nikolas really screamed loudly when he jumped off that roof, Cuspidor said.

Holly felt as if she had been punched in the stomach; the thought of her grandfather in such terror sickened her. *You killed him, didn't you?* she said.

No, I didn't kill Nikolas, said Cuspidor. *I never would have killed him without getting his blood first. But he was so scared of the flames that instead of surrendering himself to me, he jumped off the roof.* The lines that formed Cuspidor's body spun around with agitation.

You scared him. That's why he jumped, Holly said.

It doesn't matter now. He's dead, Cuspidor said.

How did you know Grandpa Nikolas was in Donkleywood? Holly asked.

He had mentioned it, said Cuspidor. *When he came to Magora, Professor Lapia informed me of his every move.*

But I thought Grandpa Nikolas never lived in Magora, Holly said.

He did—and he was very well-known here, just as you are now. They called him the Wise Man, Cuspidor said.

Grandpa Nikolas was the Wise Man? Holly asked.

She felt herself grow weaker by the minute as her blood rapidly streamed out of her body. Still lying on the ground, Holly began to move her hand slowly. Where was her brush? She had to do something. If she could only find it, she might have a chance. She searched the dirty ground next to her body and found it. She held on to the handle, but had no strength to lift it.

There was nothing more she could do. She heard Cuspidor's threatening laugh in the distance. Her eyes closed, and she drifted off into a world of colors and memories. Bits and pieces of conversations and images from her childhood flashed through her mind. Then she saw a clear picture of the day she was introduced to the unfinished rabbit. It played in her mind like a movie reeling in fast forward. There was Farouche, leaning over Holly and mumbling, "An unfinished Gindar can only use Gindar blood."

Just then, a sudden surge of energy filled Holly's entire body. As she snapped out of her stupor, she propped herself up, opened her eyes, and raised her brush.

Gindars could only use their own blood. Shaking, she staggered to her feet. If Cuspidor was sucking her blood right now, then that could mean only one thing, "I must be a Gindar," she said out loud.

Cuspidor stopped laughing. The flow of blood halted as Holly pulled it back with the newly gained energy. She stood up.

"I am a Gindar after all," Holly said confidently.

"No, not yet," said Cuspidor out loud. "You only have the right blood. You don't have the power yet to stop me."

"I might not be able to control my talent yet, but I am still a Gindar," Holly said. "Cliffony will give me the training I need to become someone special. But you will never be anything but an Unfinished without my blood!"

Cuspidor was enraged; his facial lines whirled around faster. He grabbed his brush with both hands, attempting to drain more blood from Holly. But the blood stream had stopped. Holly had gathered enough energy to stand up against Cuspidor's willpower.

With her brush in hand, Holly drew an "X" in the air.

Cuspidor stumbled back a few feet, still holding on to his brush. The thread of blood remained hovering.

Holly drew a second cross in the air.

But Cuspidor recovered from the initial hit. Holly tried a third time—without success. She wasn't strong enough. Cuspidor pulled himself together, and blood slowly began to move again along the thread.

If Holly couldn't break the thread, maybe she could apply

the Cannon Brushstroke. She aimed her brush at the rock next to Cuspidor.

Gray paint carved a large boulder out of the rock formation and shot it straight up into the crystal dome. The boulder broke a clean hole through the center without any damage to the rest of the dome. Bright rays of sunshine filled the cavern with light.

"No sunlight!" Cuspidor screamed, throwing his arms over his head.

His brush flung upward, ripping the thread of paint apart. Like the tongue of a frog pulling a fly into its mouth, the thread flicked back into Cuspidor's brush. Cuspidor screamed as if acid were being poured onto his skin. He stumbled deeper into the cavern, followed by the seahorses.

A decisive crack filled the air. Holly glanced up at the dome. Jagged fissures began to rip into the blue crystal, and she knew it was about to break.

She sped toward the tunnel and made it just before the dome collapsed. The waters of Lake Santima gushed down like a gigantic waterfall. Holly raced up the tunnel as the lake cascaded behind her. The water level rose rapidly, surging around Holly's ankles. She glanced over her shoulder and saw a wave crashing down. With her last bit of energy she made the Cannon Brushstroke again. When she turned back, she ran right into a rock and bumped her head on a stone.

She heard an avalanche of stones crash down behind her. Then she tottered, fell, and everything around her turned black.

Saying Goodbye

I would never want to live without knowing there is a fantasy world out there: A world like Magora.

Wrapped in bandages, Holly woke up in her room in Villa Nonesuch. Professor Kaplin was swinging his brush over her bruised body. Professor LePawnee peered over his shoulder. Cookie and Rufus slept on a bench opposite the bed.

"What happened?" Holly asked, still a little drowsy. She propped herself up. "Did you know that Cuspidor appeared and—"

"We know," LePawnee interrupted. "A few Ledesma butterflies remained hidden in the cavern. They brought me the message."

Cookie opened his eyes while Rufus kept sleeping.

"We are so proud of you," Cookie said.

"But all the paintings are destroyed," Holly said.

"Oh no, they are not," said Professor LePawnee. "Gate paintings are waterproof. We have already recovered most of them."

"How is Amanda?" Holly asked.

"I'm perfectly fine." Amanda peeked around the corner of the bathroom, grinning. She had a few scratches in her face, but that wasn't what surprised Holly. Amanda's long blonde hair was cut short, and she wasn't wearing any makeup.

"What happened to your hair?" Holly asked.

"I figured it would be a bit inconvenient for these kinds of adventures," said Amanda. "And I can bet that, being around you, there will be many more to come."

Holly laughed. "I hope not."

"Professor Farouche is also recovering," said LePawnee. "He should be back to normal by the end of summer break."

"I just have one more question," said Holly. "If Lapia was Cuspidor's accomplice and not Farouche, why was he with Cuspidor in Donkleywood under the oak tree?"

Brian came into the room, laughing. "I asked that same question just before you woke up."

"It was not Cuspidor behind the tree," said Professor LePawnee. "It was me."

"You?" Holly asked, bewildered.

"After we noticed that Cuspidor had entered Donkleywood, we stepped through a gate that led us behind that oak tree. We had to find you before Cuspidor did," said Professor LePawnee. "As a Ledesma, I would have attracted too much attention, so I

wore a black cloak."

"But who sent me the box? And what was Tenshi doing in that chest?" asked Holly.

"I'm not sure about that. Only your grandfather would know." LePawnee stepped to the window and flung it open. "I assume he opened a gate to the attic before his death, entered, and placed Tenshi and the brush into the chest. But I believe we will never find out for sure."

Ileana came in, holding Tenshi in her arms. "I hope you feel better," she said, placing Tenshi on Holly's comforter. The Nukimai squeaked in excitement and threw himself around Holly's neck.

"Oh I forgot—congratulations," Ileana said, handing Holly a brown bag.

Holly opened it. A dozen marzipan-griffins shot up into the air. "Thank you, Ileana. What is this for?"

"For winning the Quadrennial Art Competition," Ileana said.

"I-I-I what?" Holly stuttered.

"You won the competition. You are Cliffony's Best Artist," said Ileana. "Gina was disqualified. After the competition, the unfinished boy got a blood transfusion and was completed. He remembered that Gina cheated and attacked you. So the judges awarded you the prize."

"And now, we'll have to go back to Donkleywood," Holly said, her head drooping.

"I don't want to go back," Amanda said.

Brian scowled. "Me either. But my mom is probably awfully worried."

"I know," Holly said. "But we can't stay here forever. We are in a painting, and you know that. We have to go back to the real world."

"Right," Rufus said.

"But I expect you to return to Magora, Holly," said Professor LePawnee. "Our next school year begins in September, and I want to see you in your classes by then."

"Now, everybody out," said Professor Kaplin. "My patient needs some rest."

A week later, Holly stood in the Gallery of Wonders. The paintings were back on the walls and the whole place looked stunning. The professors, Cookie, and Ileana had gathered next to the double helix staircase to say goodbye.

"It's only for the summer," said Professor LePawnee. "We can count on you coming back in the fall, can't we?"

Holly nodded, slinging her arms around Ileana.

"Why can't you stay here?" Ileana asked.

"Our families will report us missing if we don't go back," Amanda said.

"As if, after a year, they have not already done that," Rufus said.

Cookie grinned, spun around, and once more shifted his shape. With a bang, he changed into a mirror image of Brian. Brian tumbled a step back, staring at himself, surprised.

"What are you doing, Cookie?" Holly laughed.

"I made sure that nobody would be reported missing," Cookie said.

With a bang he changed again. This time, Holly faced her twin.

"I changed into the principal of Donkleywood School," said Cookie. "As the principal, I suggested sending all four of you to boarding school—expenses paid by the school. It took some finesse to convince everybody but, in the end, your families thought you had been granted scholarships and had left for boarding school."

"My parents would never believe you unless I said goodbye to them personally," said Rufus.

"But you did say goodbye to them personally," said Cookie and with a bang he changed into Rufus. "Now they await your arrival for summer break." He changed back to his troll shape. He lifted his index finger and said, "But remember to tell everyone that you are going to boarding school, not Cliffony."

"You are hilarious," Amanda laughed and threw her arms around Cookie.

"It's time to go now," Professor LePawnee said.

Professor Gobeli clapped her hands, and a swarm of bats carried down a large painting from one of the upper staircases that crossed the gallery. The bats gently leaned it against the double helix staircase.

"Donkleywood," mumbled Holly with a resigned sigh. She did not feel like going back to the Smoralls. But at least there was one good thing about living in Donkleywood now: Ms. Hubbleworth was gone. She was stuck in Magora. But Holly worried that Ms. Hubbleworth might recover her memory and return to Donkleywood.

LePawnee swung her brush and sparkles filled the Gallery of Wonders. The gate to Donkleywood opened.

"I'll come back in the fall, Professor," Holly said. "And I'll be the best Gindar Magora has ever seen, I promise."

As she stepped into the gate, Holly glanced back once more at her new friends and smiled. Although she might have to leave for a while, she had found a home—here in Magora.

TURN THE PAGE FOR A GLIMPSE
INTO HOLLY'S NEXT JOURNEY IN

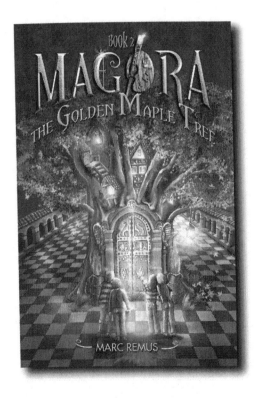

BOOK 2 - THE GOLDEN MAPLE TREE

Missing
Ms. Hubbleworth

When you paint, you create. When you write, you create. When you imagine, you create. We create every day, even when we fear we can't create anything anymore.

"Joline Hubbleworth has been missing for over a year," boomed a female voice from the widescreen TV in the Smoralls' luxurious mansion. "But the police have not yet found sufficient evidence to consider this case a crime. Jonathan Hubbleworth, husband of the seventy-two-year-old Donkleywoodian, stated today in an exclusive interview with *DonkTV News at 9* that he believes his wife must have been either kidnapped or killed. He explained further that possible suspects are plentiful because the missing person was not much appreciated in Donkleywood."

"She sure wasn't," Holly mumbled to herself, hiding behind the white leather couch in her foster parents' living room. She pulled down the knitted cap she had been wearing all the time to keep her curls under control. Why did Ms. Hubbleworth have to be so nosy? Holly sighed. If the grumpy old woman hadn't followed her into the attic, none of this would have happened.

Unlike most people in Donkleywood, Holly knew exactly where Ms. Hubbleworth was, but she kept quiet because her foster parents, the Smoralls, would have locked her up in the attic if she told the truth. Nobody would have listened to a twelve-year-old anyhow.

A year ago, Holly had jumped into a fantasy painting that had been created by her grandfather, Nikolas. Ms. Hubbleworth had been sticking her nose where it didn't belong when she accidentally tripped into the same painting. Even if Holly told the authorities, nobody would believe that Ms. Hubbleworth was alive and currently teaching art in a magical world called Magora. Nobody would have believed Holly but three other children: Brian, Rufus, and Amanda. They had followed Holly into the painting and attended Cliffony, Academy of the Arts, for a full year. There, they had learned to paint with the help of magic.

"Strange sightings have been reported on a regular basis," continued the TV reporter.

Holly peeked out from behind the leather couch and glanced past the orangutan-like heads of Mr. Smorall and his daughter, Barb.

"Numerous witnesses have claimed that flying seahorses the size of cats have been seen in Donkleywood over the past year," said the reporter. "The police call it mass hysteria. Nevertheless, we cannot discount the fact that over forty-five people have reported these creatures that are said to be hovering in thin air."

Holly pressed her hand over her mouth so she would not let out a sound. The seahorses were still on the loose. Holly knew that this was not mass hysteria. These creatures were the helpers of an evil creature called S.A. Lokin, the Duke of Cuspidor. In Magora, Holly had come face-to-face with him. She had found out that he was one of the so-called Unfinished, creatures that had not been completed by a master painter.

"DonkTV will have a special report on the seahorse sightings tomorrow night, right after the *News at 9*," said the reporter. "Please join us tomorrow for…"

Holly didn't hear the end of the sentence. She felt the dust behind the couch tickle her nose. Like a volcanic eruption, a loud sneeze shook her whole body. Three fuming faces turned her way.

"What are you doing down there, loser?" Barb asked.

Ms. Smorall's giant hawk-like nose turned red, and the color spread to her cheeks. She let out a high-pitched scream and yelled, "Out of here! I've told you a million times you're not allowed in the living room. Back to the attic right now!"

She jumped up from the leather recliner, leaped toward Holly, and grabbed her by the ear.

"Don't make such a fuss about it, hon," said Mr. Smorall. "Holly is not worth getting worked up about."

"She's not allowed in here, Herbert," said Ms. Smorall. "You know exactly what a troublemaker she is. Even her teachers know she's living in a fantasy world. Back at Donkleywood School she never focused on her work. All she did was scribble everywhere."

"They are not scribbles," said Holly. "They are drawings. I'm a good artist. I even won—"

Holly stopped in the middle of the sentence. She had won the title of "Best Artist" in Magora, but since Ms. Smorall did not know anything about that fantasy world, it would only make things worse if Holly let that slip.

Ms. Smorall's face turned red. "You are anything but an artist," she yelled.

"But hon, what if she has some talent?" Mr. Smorall asked.

Holly noticed sudden panic on Ms. Smorall's face. Nervously, she pushed Holly out of the living room.

To Holly's surprise, Ms. Smorall whispered in an almost caring tone, "You'd better go now." Then, she spun around and screeched, "Herbert, darling, how could you even think that Holly has a spark of talent? You know how bad she is in the arts."

Mr. Smorall grunted and turned back to the news. Ms. Smorall slammed the living room door shut.

A few more weeks and Holly would not have to listen this anymore. She was going back to Magora for her second year of studies at Cliffony, Academy of the Arts.

She trudged down the hallway, thinking how it would be to have caring parents like everyone else. Occasionally, Ms.

Smorall seemed friendly, but every time Mr. Smorall appeared she started screaming and acted as if she hated Holly from the bottom of her heart. Mr. Smorall was less vocal, but that was exactly what drove Holly crazy. She could deal with Ms. Smorall's verbal and physical outbursts, but she couldn't deal with the fact that Mr. Smorall treated her as if she were invisible.

After the death of her parents, Holly had lived most of her life with Grandpa Nikolas. And since he had been like a father to her until he died in a horrible fire last year, she missed having a dad more than a mom. Holly sat down on the marble staircase and thought about some of her friends she had met in Magora. There was Ileana, a former Unfinished who had just been completed through blood donations, and Cookie, the shape-shifter, who took care of the kids in the living tree house where they stayed, Villa Nonesuch.

"I have to get back to Magora," she mumbled. Even though it wasn't the real world, it had become her home now, and Cookie, Villa Nonesuch, and Ileana were a much better family than the Smoralls."

A sizzling sound echoed through the hallway and interrupted Holly's thoughts. She snapped out of her daydream and jumped up. What was that? The sizzling echoed again. Holly tiptoed back down the hallway until she reached Mr. Smorall's office.

She had never set a foot in the office before because it was off limits to her. Not that she had ever wanted to go inside, but this time was different. The sizzling seemed familiar to Holly, but she could not remember where she had heard it before. Carefully, she opened the door. There was a massive desk in the middle of the wood-paneled office. On the left was a fireplace, and on the right were bookshelves filled with papers and ring binders. Behind the desk was an open window. It banged violently against the shelves.

Relieved, Holly went to the window and closed it. It was nothing but the wind.

With a decisive slam, the door flew shut behind her, and Holly felt hot breath on the back of her neck. She spun around and stared into four blazing red eyes.

"S-s-seahorses," stuttered Holly, tumbling backward.

The two seahorses were covered in rusted armor and had spiked needles on their tails. Holly knew they were not to be messed with.

At that precise moment, a humming filled the air. Out of the corner of her eye, Holly saw a bright light forming in the air in front of the fireplace. The seahorses flinched. The rectangle increased in size, and within seconds, an entrance had opened up.

"Jeepers. A gate," said Holly, gaping at the light-filled opening. "Someone is coming from Magora."

A *whoosh* indicated that someone was on the way. A bright flash of light exploded from the gate, and there in front of Holly was a huge creature, wrapped in a black hooded cloak.

Holly wanted to let out a scream, but the sound got stuck in her throat. She began to breathe heavily and stuttered, "C-c-cuspidor."

The hooded creature leaned forward menacingly. Holly slid down to the floor and squeezed her eyes shut. It was all over now.

Marc Remus is an award-winning German Neo Pop-Art painter and illustrator with exhibitions world-wide. He was educated in the United States, graduated with a BA in art and illustration from Art Center College of Design in Pasadena, CA, and lived in Japan and Central America for some years. He has travelled to more than sixty countries and visited over a thousand cities, of which he has painted over two hundred. His work has been featured on TV and in many magazines and newspapers in Germany, USA, and Mexico.

During his studies in California, Remus took his first children's book illustration class. His teacher inspired him to start writing and not just illustrating. The result was a picture book called *Painting Brian*, which led to the *Magora* series. Over a period of twenty years, Remus has developed this magical world based on places he has visited, people he has met, and things he has learned through his studies in acting, cultural Anthropology, and linguistics.

He continues to have painting exhibitions, studies Mandarin and Spanish, and enjoys travelling the world.

Visit the website and sign up to get the latest news on Magora:
www.MarcRemus.com/author

ACKNOWLEDGEMENTS

I AM GRATEFUL to Melinda Fassett-Welles for her early support, many years ago, when she introduced me to the fascinating world of children's literature. I will always remember her kindness as I made the first uncertain steps. May she rest in peace!

I wish to thank Nancy Butts for teaching me the foundation of writing and for helping me edit the series from the very beginning. She has been a bountiful treasure of knowledge and a good friend over all the years. I couldn't have done it without you!

I am honored to have had the opportunity to work with award-winning poet and writer Ardath Mayhar. She helped me edit an early draft of this volume and gave me much needed-advice. May she rest in peace, as well!

I appreciate the meticulous reading and copyediting by Marlo Garnsworthy and the eagle eye of Crystal Watanabe. You made the series shine.

Thanks also to Troon Harrison for having started working with me on Magora. I wish we could have continued working together.

Many people were involved with the series, though not directly with the writing. Among them: Brian Sutow, who did a fantastic job recording the first three chapters for the audio book; Jun Park, who created a stunning intro animation; Patrick Rundblad for creating the magical soundtrack for the website; Morten Gulliksen for breathing life into Tenshi; and James Li for translating parts of the volume into Mandarin Chinese.

I am grateful to the many friends who read versions of this book as it was taking shape. Damaris not only gave a character her name but also offered me much-needed advice on an early version. Dave kindly read and responded to the first volume, which helped improve the book tremendously. Ingo gave one of the professors his last name and he supported me a lot. Alyssa, Andy, Elisabeth, Ian, Jenny, Katja, and Tonya all read this volume and gave me helpful feedback. I appreciate your support.

A special thanks to Sylke for not only lending her name to an entire species in Magora but for having been such a good friend over the decades.

I wish to thank the many kids who read the books with such enthusiasm and passion and pushed me to complete the series, among them Aryana, Sofia, Gigi, Haley, Isabella, Lena & Lena, Susana, and Zoey.

Thanks to my parents and my entire family in the US, Germany, and France for their unshakable faith in me, and especially to my mother for reactivating her English skills to read the series.

Finally, I wish to thank Nikolas for having been a fantastic teacher so many years ago and for making Magora, its characters, and places come alive. You will always have a special place in my heart.

The Gallery of Wonders has won the following literary awards:

GOLD MEDALS:

Moonbeam Children's Book Award.
Gold medal winner in the
"Pre-Teen Fiction Ebook" category, 2016.

SILVER MEDALS:

Independent Publisher Book Award (IPPY)
Silver Medal Winner in the "Juvenile Fiction" category, 2016.

Readers' Favorite Award
Silver Medal Winner in the
"Children's Fantasy/ Sci-Fi" category, 2016

Purple Dragonfly Award
Second place in the "Middle Grade Fiction" category, 2016

FINALIST:

International Book Awards
Finalist in the "Children's Fiction" category, 2016.

National Indie Excellence Awards (NIEA)
Finalist in the "Pre-Teen Fiction" category, 2016.

NABE Pinnacle Book Achievement Award
Best book in the "Juvenile Fiction" category, Winter 2016.

63322497R00163

Made in the USA
Charleston, SC
02 November 2016